Bride of the Barrier Master

2

Kureha

YEN ON

NEW YORK

Bride of the Barrier Master 2

KUREHA

Translation by Linda Liu ◆ Cover art by Bodax

KEKKAISHI NO ICHIRINKA Vol.2
©Kureha 2022
First published in Japan in 2022 by KADOKAWA CORPORATION, Tokyo.
English translation rights arranged with KADOKAWA CORPORATION, Tokyo, through TUTTLE-MORI AGENCY, INC., Tokyo.

English translation © 2023 by Yen Press, LLC

Yen On
150 West 30th Street, 19th Floor
New York, NY 10001

Visit us at yenpress.com
facebook.com/yenpress
twitter.com/yenpress
yenpress.tumblr.com
instagram.com/yenpress

First Yen On Edition: August 2023
Edited by Yen On Editorial: Leilah Labossiere
Designed by Yen Press Design: Madelaine Norman

Yen On is an imprint of Yen Press, LLC.
The Yen On name and logo are trademarks of Yen Press, LLC.

Library of Congress Cataloging-in-Publication Data
Names: Kureha (Light novel author), author. | Liu, Linda (Translator), translator.
Title: Bride of the barrier master / Kureha ; translation by Linda Liu.
Other titles: Kekkaishi no ichirinka. English
Description: First Yen On edition. | New York : Yen On, 2023–
Identifiers: LCCN 2022043316 | ISBN 9781975360528 (v. 1 ; trade paperback) |
    ISBN 9781975370336 (v. 2 ; trade paperback)
Subjects: LCGFT: Fantasy fiction. | Romance fiction. | Light novels.
Classification: LCC PZ7.1.K85 Br 2023 | DDC [Fic]—dc23
LC record available at https://lccn.loc.gov/2022043316

ISBNs: 978-1-9753-7033-6 (paperback)
        978-1-9753-7034-3 (ebook)

10 9 8 7 6 5 4 3 2 1

LSC-C

Printed in the United States of America

Contents

Prologue

The Association of Practitioners.

The Association was established by the five great clans who were charged with the protection of the pillars, and it had branches throughout the country.

Its headquarters was under the jurisdiction of the Ichinomiya clan and was more tightly guarded than the main Ichinomiya residence. It was a place that was difficult to set foot in—even for practitioners if they weren't registered with the Association—and was, needless to say, strictly off-limits to the common person.

Within it slept spelled talismans kept hidden from the world.

Four of the clans each had their own specialties.

Nijouin specialized in the creation of spelled talismans.

Sankourou were experts at defense; Yotsukado, the masters of offense.

Goyougi excelled at curses.

Incidentally, the Ichinomiya clan was well-rounded in all of those skills. Sure, it was merely one of the five clans, but as the clan with the highest number of talented practitioners, it was also the most influential.

That was why the Association's headquarters, where dangerous talismans crafted by the Nijouin were held, fell under the Ichinomi-yas' jurisdiction.

Nonetheless, the Association was made up of all five clans, and the responsibility of its management was shared equally. The headquarters stood at the head of every branch—its security was tighter than any-where else.

No protection measures were spared. The Nijouins' talismans were one reason for that. And yet...

One day, intruders broke into the Association's headquarters.

It was unclear how they were able to penetrate the facility's airtight defenses.

The alarm blared through the headquarters' halls, and every practi-tioner in the building scrambled to find the culprits.

"Where are they? Where did they go?!"

"What's going on with the security cameras?"

"Seal off the exits!"

"First, protect the top-security vault!"

Amid the cacophony of shouts, practitioners ran for the most impor-tant of the headquarters' vaults.

Normally, its gate was bolted and locked. However, the group arrived to find it gaping wide-open.

The blood drained from their faces.

They shouted for backup before cautiously entering the vault in case the intruders were still inside.

But there was neither hide nor hair of the criminals to be seen.

At a glance, it looked as if nothing had been touched, but when they went through the room item by item, they realized several talismans were missing.

Furthermore, among all the talismans kept in the vault, each and every one of the missing items was classified as particularly dangerous.

The thieves had only taken the most preciously guarded items, yet there were no signs of rummaging or ransacking. It was as if they had known exactly where their targets would be, snapped them up without a glance at anything else, and made their escape.

"How could this have happened...?"

"To think, of all things, *those* talismans were stolen. What a fiasco."

At a loss, the practitioners came to a standstill.

"We don't have the time for this."

"We must report to the heads of the five clans immediately!"

"They couldn't have gotten very far yet! All hands on deck! Find those thieves!"

But the intruders were not found.

However, one of the practitioners at the scene noticed something in the vault and picked it up.

It was a button decorated with a distinctive motif.

Chapter 1

The atmosphere in the Ichise household had been frigid as of late, ever since Hana, the younger daughter of the family, had been chosen to be the clan head's wife.

All her life, Hana had been compared with her brilliant older sister, Hazuki, and found lacking. She was the older sister's scraps, worthless and good-for-nothing. Though Hazuki had borne the weight and responsibility of the family's expectations, Hana had left her sister behind and become the mistress of the clan herself.

Her parents couldn't believe it. When in the world had she even met the head of the clan? They nursed resentment toward Hana.

What grated on them more than anything was Hana's continued disregard for the family.

As the mistress of the clan, she could surely bestow some favor on her own family, and yet though the Ichises had raised the newlywed bride, their standing within the branch families was just as low as ever.

Hana's parents couldn't stand it.

Even when they went to the Ichinomiya residence to meet with Hana, they were turned away at the door.

Apparently, there were restrictions on who was allowed to speak to Hana, as per the orders of the clan head, Saku Ichinomiya.

They were Hana's parents, but they hadn't been able to get a word in when the marriage had been decided upon. They were furious at the cold-shoulder treatment, but they were steadfastly ignored.

"What happened to the letter you sent Hana, dear?" Hana's mother asked one day.

"It was returned with the envelope unopened," her father answered.

"My word! How could she?"

"Shit! That ungrateful child! Why did she turn out this way? Hazuki does what we tell her to. She's such a dutiful child. How can they be twins? Hazuki is doubtlessly the better match for the head of the clan, and yet he ignored the feast before his eyes and chose the scraps!"

Horrible words from people who had never given Hana the time of day.

Had they raised her with love and warmth, she would have grown up obeying her parents and would've returned their attention with affection, of course. She would have made sure her family was provided for and raised their standing.

But that hadn't been the reality. Her parents had only had eyes for Hazuki and didn't care for Hana in the slightest. Hana had spent every day of her life scorned and ridiculed.

"*If only you had doted on your younger daughter more,*" sneered people from equally low-ranked families while suppressing their mocking laughter.

They would spitefully add, "*All that time and effort poured into the elder twin's education has gone down the drain,*" using Hazuki to throw a jab at the two parents who had placed all their hopes on their older daughter.

Now the twins' parents could only grit their teeth and say nothing in response. The one thing they had in excess was their useless pride.

And for some reason, they aimed all their resentment toward Hana. Everything was that good-for-nothing's fault.

However, there was no satisfaction to be found there since they could not meet her.

They had no choice but to come up with an alternate plan to restore their family's standing.

Plan B took the shape of a leather folio, currently lying on the table in front of Hazuki's father.

"This is the only option we have remaining to raise our status to where it once was," he said, his resolute gaze fixed on the folio.

Hazuki was called into the room, where both her parents were waiting with serious expressions.

"Pardon me," she said when she entered. "Father. Mother. You have some business with me?"

While Hazuki looked like her younger sister, her features held a certain allure. If she noticed the abnormal atmosphere in the room, she didn't say anything about it.

However, her face was wan, perhaps because she felt ill at ease.

"Good of you to come, Hazuki. Sit," her father said. He was wearing an exaggerated smile.

Hazuki was discomfited by her father's expression but did as she was told and sat down facing her parents.

The moment she did, her father threw a compliment her way. "You are truly an excellent daughter, Hazuki. We heard you scored the highest in your grade on the recent exam, no?"

"Thank you." Hazuki bowed her head, her expression unchanged.

He continued to flatter her. "Ever since you were a child, you have always been brilliant. You even summoned a human shikigami. We have always been proud that you are our daughter."

"What has brought this on all of a sudden, Father?" Hazuki asked, troubled by the praise her father normally never bothered with.

"Nothing. I have only been reminded of how pleased we are that you grew up just the way we wanted you to." He placed the brown album in front of Hazuki. "Open it."

"Wha—? All right..." She followed her father's instructions and opened the album. Inside was a large photo of a man, one she'd seen but never spoken to before. "What is this photo for?" she asked, her stomach sinking.

The picture folio looked like the ones prepared for arranged marriages. *But that can't be*, Hazuki tried to reassure herself.

However, her father's reply confirmed her premonition. "We have found you a husband."

"We received a favorable response from the other party just recently. Isn't that wonderful, Hazuki?" her mother said.

The thought that their daughter would be anything but overjoyed never crossed their minds.

Hazuki protested reflexively, "Please wait! As I recall, this man is in his forties. There is too much of an age gap. In addition—!"

Her father cut off the rest of her complaints with a sharp rebuke. "What of it?" he barked. "Age is a trivial matter. What is important is whether the marriage will benefit the family. That is it."

"......" Hazuki's lips drew tight, and she didn't argue further.

Her parents had a habit of turning a deaf ear to her opinion when it came to what was favorable for the family. It had been this way long before that day, and their disregard stole the words from her mouth.

"Don't tell me you want to marry for love," her father scoffed. "You know better than to say such foolish things, right, Hazuki?"

"...Yes, Father."

Hazuki's acquiescence immediately brought a smile to her father's face.

"You must understand, Hazuki, this marriage is a vital step for our family," her mother added.

"I understand..."

"If only Hana was competent, I wouldn't have had to beg like this," her father spat. "What a worthless daughter she turned out to be. How can twins be so different from each other? It's a relief that you are such an outstanding child and have always met our expectations."

Hazuki forced a smile onto her face and clenched the fist resting on her thigh to restrain herself.

Her parents were in a celebratory mood and didn't notice a thing.

"Formal introductions will be made later on. Until then, conduct yourself properly so as not to disgrace this household. Well, I'm sure I hardly need to tell you that at your age," her father said.

"That's right, dear. Hazuki wouldn't defy her parents and act like a fool. She's modest and obedient, unlike Hana," her mother said. "She exemplifies the traits of a perfect Japanese lady."

The pair extolled Hazuki's virtues and decried Hana's faults in the same breath, both unaware that there could be anything wrong with the way they were talking.

They were praising Hazuki by comparing her with Hana on the surface, but in reality, they were shackling Hazuki down. Surely, they realized that much.

Children who listened to their parents were good. Children who didn't were bad. Part of Hazuki was repulsed by her parents' way of thinking.

Every time Hana's name was mentioned, every time they were compared, the burden of being the ideal daughter grew heavier.

Her other half. That invaluable fragment.

When had their paths diverged?

No one—not even Hana herself, most likely—knew how sad Hazuki felt hearing her parents call Hana worthless.

As long as she pushed herself hard enough and even took on Hana's share, she could please her parents, and they would cease their derogations of Hana.

As long as she stayed the golden child...

When had doing as her parents said become second nature? When had she become unable to rebel?

She had become too conscious of what others thought of her and had continued to play the role of the perfect honor student all this time.

It was suffocating, but that was something she could no longer confess.

In the past, when she and Hana had still gotten along, Hazuki had often troubled Hana with her complaints. What she found most agonizing and sad was the distance between them that had grown over the years. Although she had behaved the way she had for Hana's sake, in the end, her actions had created the gulf between them.

How had she ended up here?

Hazuki no longer had any idea.

Everything had backfired. Hana, whom she had intended to protect, had left her side. Hazuki was alone.

Help me. Someone. Anyone.

The plea that resided in her heart remained unspoken.

◆

A short while after the inugami incident, once the wounds Hana had sustained during the final confrontation had healed, Saku, her husband and the head of the Ichinomiya clan, came to her with an invitation.

He wanted to show her the oceanside villa that was her reward for assisting on the case.

The bite from the inugami had left a gnarled scar that was unlikely to ever disappear completely, according to the doctor.

Hana counted herself lucky that she'd survived the showdown against the tatarigami with only some minor scarring. However, in contrast to her optimistic outlook, Arashi, the inugami in question and her new shikigami, grew despondent every time he saw the wound, so she had stopped wearing sleeveless clothing that revealed the scar.

Nonetheless, that was a small price to pay to keep Arashi's spirits up.

Occasionally, she was still struck with cramping pain from the scar, so her concerned shikigami tried to stop her from going to see the villa. However, the wound didn't hurt enough that she'd turn down the golden opportunity Saku had offered. She accepted his invitation with glee.

Their final destination turned out to be a coastal town a two-hour drive from the Ichinomiya residence.

"Wow, amazing! It's the ocean! The real deal!" Hana cried, leaning out the car window. The smell of salt water rode in on the wind whipping around her face. It was a scent that she rarely got to smell, and it invigorated her.

"Careful! It's dangerous to stick your face out the window like that," chided Saku, unfazed by the sight of the ocean.

"'Kaaay." Hana obediently settled back in her seat.

Hana's butterfly shikigami, Azuha, left her usual perch on Hana's hair to flutter excitedly around the car. "Master, that's the ocean?" she asked childishly.

"Oh yeah…you've never seen the ocean before," Hana mused.

"Nope."

Hana didn't visit the shore often, but she'd gone a few times, once for a school outing in elementary school to a beach nearby and once on an overnight trip during middle school, if she recalled correctly.

Both had been regular schools, so she hadn't been able to bring Azuha—a shikigami—with her.

The Ichises weren't the kind of chummy family that went on trips together, either. It had been a long time since Hana had traveled as far as the ocean.

She was far more fired up than the situation demanded, but she hoped anyone watching would pretend otherwise.

The villa was not just next to the ocean; it was situated on a hill with an impressive view of the water.

It may have been set a little far from the actual beach, but the view was to die for.

On top of that, it was originally one of the Ichinomiyas' properties, meaning the grounds were so massive that it was impossible to see how far they extended from the front gate.

The car pulled to a stop in front of the gate. Hana gazed out the window with wide eyes, taking everything in, barely able to sit still in her seat.

Saku watched her exasperatedly. "Get a hold of yourself. The villa's not going anywhere."

"I know, I know. I'm just looking forward to it," she replied. "Are you sure I can have this entire place?" They hadn't gone inside yet, but judging from the grand gate, it was sure to be impressive. She was already beside herself with excitement.

"Yeah, I promised. Your name is already on the deed, so by every definition, it's your villa."

She smiled widely and threw both hands into the air. "Yes! Thanks, Saku!"

The corner of Saku's mouth curled upward in a mischievous grin. "Why don't you show your appreciation with actions instead of words?"

"What do you mean?" Hana said, a foreboding feeling washing over her.

Saku leaned over, caging her in with his arms.

She panicked and began to protest. "W-wait! You're too close!"

"Get used to it already, you airhead." His smile grew bold, and he grabbed her chin with one hand. "Have you fallen for my charms?"

His lips were a breath away from hers. She flushed as red as a tomato.

They had been required to marry so that Saku could restore the barrier around the pillar, but even now that the barrier was back at full strength, they remained husband and wife. Saku had had a change of heart.

He had played dirty, but surprisingly, they were getting along.

Now that she had the backing of the Ichinomiyas, there was nothing more that Hana—who had left her family and had no one to rely on—could wish for.

At first, she had been shunned by the Ichinomiyas, but once she had revealed the existence of Aoi and Miyabi, her two human shikigami, she had gained the acceptance of not only the household's servants, but also the lady of the family as well, Saku's mother. Truth be told, her current lifestyle was far from uncomfortable.

Back at the Ichise house, she had eaten every meal alone, but now she took meals together with the Ichinomiyas.

At first, she had been reluctant. She had thought that eating alone was less of a hassle. Making small talk over dinner put her on edge, but at the same time, the food tasted more delicious.

Was this what she had been wishing for all along? To be part of a warm family?

Anyway, at the end of the day, she didn't object to living in the Ichinomiya residence. Her objection was to Saku.

She was only his wife because of a legal contract, and yet Saku—whose very forward advances didn't stop at kisses—had gotten even more handsy since it was decided they would stay married. He took every opportunity to steal a kiss, sneak his arm around her shoulder, or embrace her. Hana was inexperienced when it came to affairs of the heart and was at his mercy.

At times like this when Saku pressed close, his gaze intent, Hana had her trusty shikigami to watch her back.

"HEY! What the hell do you think you're doing to my master, you perverted geezer?!" one of those shikigami shouted with a growl, cursing like a gangster. He wrenched open the door and kicked Saku away from Hana.

The shikigami's name was Aoi, and a great sword was strapped to his back.

Next, Miyabi—beautiful as an angel—took Hana by the hand and helped her out of the car. "Master, please come this way."

The two were somewhat overprotective of Hana, to say the least.

"Thanks, Aoi, Miyabi," Hana said, relieved.

She peeked into the car. Saku lay in a heap where he had fallen. Dissatisfaction was written clearly across his face. "You two again," he said with a tsk.

"That's our line!" Aoi retorted. "You're harassing her!"

"I was seducing her," corrected Saku. "Outsiders should butt out. This is a problem between a husband and his wife."

"'Husband and wife,' my ass. You tricked her! You have no right to talk!" Aoi spat back, snapping at Saku's throat like Hana's personal guard dog.

Arashi, who took the form of an actual dog, materialized as well. "As your shikigami, should I back Aoi up?" he asked Hana, a bit bewildered.

"No, it's okay, Arashi. It wouldn't be a game anymore if a god was to step in," she said.

Arashi looked like a lovable black puppy, but he was actually an inugami, a dog deity. If he used his full power against Saku, Saku's life would be in danger.

"Aha, I see. They're playing a game. That's what you call a lover's spat, right?" With sincere admiration, Arashi watched Aoi and Saku have it out. He was somewhat oblivious when it came to the human world, and Hana could only smile wryly at him.

"Stop fooling around," she called to the boys who were bickering across the threshold of the car. "I want to hurry and see what my new villa is like."

Saku and Aoi finally stopped arguing and turned their attention to Hana.

"You're right. We have to clean up before it gets dark," Saku said. He climbed out of the car and dusted off Aoi's footprint from his clothes.

Saku normally wore traditional Japanese attire around the Ichinomiya residence, but today, he'd put on a casual outfit of jeans and a basic shirt.

Hana was dressed in cropped pants and a floral blouse—it seemed important to wear clothing that was easy to move around in.

"Huh? It hasn't been cleaned?" Hana asked.

"The inside is immaculate," answered Saku. "The outside is the problem."

"What? The lawn needs mowing?"

"You'll see when we get there," he said cryptically.

The Ichinomiya servants who had followed them in a separate car opened the front gate. They had likely come as aids.

"Come, let's go." Saku strode forward quickly, leaving Hana and her shikigami scrambling to catch up.

Strangely enough, the servants remained at the gate.

Hana asked, "Hey, Saku, what about them?"

"They'll come after we're done," came the reply.

"Eh? Wouldn't cleaning be part of their job, normally?"

How could the staff of the Ichinomiya household make the lord of the clan clean? Shouldn't it have been the opposite?

But Hana's questions were quickly answered.

After a five-minute walk from the gate, they saw a beautiful western-style house far too large and lavish for Hana and her shikigami to live in alone. On top of that, the grounds were massive. A person could hit golf balls here to their heart's content. Its luxury far exceeded Hana's expectations. Anyone who saw it would be struck with admiration for the Ichinomiya family.

However, there was one trait that stood out far more than the house itself: droves of *somethings* wandered around as they pleased.

The picturesque vista was ruined by shades, shades, and more shades. Shades everywhere you looked.

"What the hell is this?!" Hana screamed the moment she saw what was waiting for them, and who could blame her? "Sakuuu! Care to explain?!" she demanded furiously.

Saku replied as if nothing was wrong, "They're shades, as you can see."

"Oh, shades, of course. NOT! Why are they here?"

"Ah. This villa has become—for a variety of reasons—a regular gathering spot for shades. They have to be cleaned up regularly."

"Cleaned…"

The meaning of "cleaning" dawned on Hana, and she now understood why the servants hadn't joined them.

It was only natural. Most of the servants would have come from practitioner families, but regardless, had they the power to take down shades, they would have become practitioners instead of household staff.

Saku continued, "The shades here are not only excessive in numbers, but they're powerful as well, so it's not a job that can be entrusted to an incompetent practitioner. Up until now, I've visited once in a while to deal with them, but then you came along talking about compensation. A match made in heaven, I'd say."

"Exchange! I'd like to request an exchange! I want a different villa!" Hana cried.

"Give it up. The paperwork is already done. It's yours now, so you better maintain it properly."

"Y-you tricked me..." Hana dropped to her knees, her shoulders slumping.

Her sheer excitement at the idea of owning a villa made the shock of the betrayal even greater. It was too devastating a blow to bounce back from quickly. She paid no mind to the fact that her white pants had been dirtied by sand.

But neither Saku nor the shades showed any consideration for her broken heart.

"Get up, Hana. They're coming," Saku said. He rolled up his sleeves as if to pump himself up for the work ahead and summoned his shikigami. "Tsubaki. Come."

"All righty!" A girl in a frilly maid costume materialized. Her white hair was tied up in pigtails, and dog ears popped out of her head. She was Saku's human shikigami, Tsubaki.

The moment she appeared, she zeroed in on Aoi. "Omigosh, it's my darling!"

"Ngh—!" Her predatory gaze spooked Aoi.

Tsubaki used to introduce herself as Saku's lover, but she had fallen in love with Aoi at first sight and no longer had eyes for anyone else.

She looked ready to pounce on Aoi at any second, but Saku grabbed her by the top of her head. "Save your darling for later. You can go on all the dates you want after we clean this up," he said.

"Yes! You can count on me! Don't go anywhere, darling!" You could practically hear a heart emoji tacked on at the end of her every sentence.

Tsubaki blew a kiss in Aoi's direction before launching herself into the horde of shades.

Revolted by the air kiss, Aoi paled. He turned a pleading look toward Hana. "Help, Master. I don't know how to deal with that woman…"

But Hana was the one who wanted to be rescued. She had no time to think about Aoi's plight. "Cruel. So cruel. I was looking forward to it. I poured all my energy into resolving the case for the sake of this villa, and this is how you repay me…"

She turned to glare at the shades that had the gall to attack her while she was on the verge of tears and screamed, "Give me back my villa!" She vented her anger on the inconsiderate shades. "Expand! Expand! Expand!" she yelled, trapping the shades in succession. "Eliminate!!!" Her final command was a war cry, and with it, she destroyed the nearby shades all in one go.

"Aoi, Miyabi, Azuha! Exterminate the intruders that dared to come to my house uninvited," she ordered her shikigami.

"Shall I help, too?" Arashi asked.

"Please. You are as powerful as an army of a hundred men."

"Yes."

Arashi, unfazed by the shades, dashed into the fray. Aoi followed after him.

"Let's see who can take down more of them, Arashi," Aoi called.

"Fine by me. I won't lose," replied Arashi.

"That's my line."

The two of them kept up the friendly banter as they ran off.

Hana watched them go and huffed peevishly. "Hmph. This isn't the time to goof around."

"Master, you've become quite inconsolable," Miyabi said, frowning in concern.

Well, who wouldn't despair in a situation like that?

"Saku, you bastard! Don't think I'm gonna forget this!" Hana screamed.

What was she to do with the anger welling up inside her?

For the time being, she decided to unleash her fury on the shades. One after another, they were consumed by the fires of her anger.

◆

Saku looked on with admiration. "I knew it was the right decision to have her deal with them."

It was laughable how quickly Hana, burning with rage, was mowing down the shades.

The Ichinomiya family had owned this villa and had been looking after it for generations.

The shades here were strong, unlike the small fries that manifested elsewhere, and it took multiple skilled practitioners to clear them out. However, requisitioning multiple practitioners on a regular basis was out of the question, so up until now, Saku had dealt with the problem himself.

It was a large job that took him the whole day, but Hana had the inugami Arashi on her side, and before their might, the shades melted away.

Watching the scene, Saku felt a weight lift off his shoulders.

Ever since he'd become the head of the clan, he hadn't been able to take time out of his schedule like before. It was a blessing to be able to entrust this villa to Hana.

◆

In the end, they managed to wipe out the shades on the grounds before noon. Once the servants heard it was clear, they swarmed in.

Hana lay collapsed on a bench in the garden. "I'm exhausted...," she grumbled. To blow off steam, she had pushed her body to its limits, and as a result, she was groggy. She didn't want to take another step.

In contrast, the shikigami were bursting with energy. Shikigami were formed from their master's power, and *tired* wasn't in their vocabulary.

"Aw man, it's my loss," Aoi said after his shade-hunting competition with Arashi.

"You were a worthy opponent," Arashi replied.

Tsubaki flounced in between them and draped herself over Aoi. "You were amazing, darling. As a reward, I'll take you out on a date!"

"Gyaaah!" Aoi shrieked. "Nope. Not necessary!"

"Come on now, there's no need to be shy," she purred.

"I'm not being shy! Get offa me!"

"Nooope."

Hana watched Aoi's and Tsubaki's ruckus with resignation from where she was lying on the bench, her head pillowed on Miyabi's lap. Miyabi looked on with a smile. Azuha was flitting cheerfully around the garden, making a tour of the flowers in bloom.

What a carefree bunch of shikigami.

"It's so lively," Hana muttered.

The scene before her was completely different from her life with the Ichises.

Aoi and Miyabi could manifest as they pleased without worrying about who was watching, and to Hana, they looked like they were more energetic than ever.

She had thought she'd made a major blunder by entering this contractual marriage to Saku, but for Aoi and Miyabi, who had led a life in hiding, it might have been the right choice.

While she was relaxing on the bench, Saku walked over, calling for her. "Hana, everything's squared away inside. There aren't any signs of shades, either, so you can go in now."

Hana trained a stony gaze on Saku, who didn't seem to feel even a grain of remorse for dragging Hana into this mess.

"You cheater."

She had tons of things she wanted to say, but her anger had crested, and the scathing critique she had for him had dried up. Instead, she glared daggers at him.

"That's slander," Saku said. "It's a villa, isn't it? It overlooks the ocean, doesn't it? I didn't lie."

"If I'd known it was a hangout spot for shades, I wouldn't have accepted it!" Hana protested with wide eyes. Her shouting had no effect on Saku.

"It wasn't anything you would've wanted to hear."

"Of course not, idiot!"

Who on earth would want a murder mansion filled with shades?

"Would *you* have wanted it?" Hana demanded.

"Nah, no thanks," replied Saku.

Faced with his indifference, Hana lost the energy to yell. She sighed deeply and steadied herself before standing up from the bench. "I can go in?"

"Yeah. Lunch is ready. Let's go eat."

"Fine, fine."

Clearly irritated, she trailed behind him into the western-style building.

On the inside, it was so luxuriously decorated, one wouldn't have thought it was a mere villa. Unlike the quiet and refined atmosphere of the Ichinomiya residence, which was a traditional Japanese dwelling, the furnishings and interior design were vibrant and gave the building a bright and cheery atmosphere.

Hana assumed that she'd be given a villa that was hardly used, but the building had been properly maintained and didn't look old at all.

"The weather's nice today, so I had them set up lunch on the terrace," Saku told her.

The wide terrace commanded a panoramic view of the ocean. When she saw it, she gasped. "Wow, it's beautiful."

"Isn't it? Location-wise, it's top-notch."

She knew exactly what he was implying. Had there not been any shades here, this villa would have been a five-star property.

Leave it to shades to ruin everything. That was all there was to say about that.

"If only it was shade-free," Hana said.

"Yeah. But with your power, you'll manage."

"Sure, I'll *manage*, but I won't be able to take care of it once I get old, you know?"

"The clan will repossess it when that time comes. In the meantime, I'm counting on you to maintain it for me. There aren't any other properties I can give you, and I have my duties as the clan head to oversee. I don't have time to spend on this villa."

"Can't be helped," Hana drawled. "Because I'm sooo generous, I'll do you a favor and clean it up once in a while."

Saku's responsibilities as the lord of the clan piled on top of his work as a practitioner. She compromised this time for his sake.

Saku smiled softly. "That'll be a great help."

Hana found herself smiling back at him. "FYI, the next time you pull a scam like this, I'm divorcing you on the spot."

"No worries. With my authority as the leader of the clan, I'll crush any such declarations without mercy."

"Accept it with grace!"

"Don't want to."

What an egomaniac he was.

The problem was…Hana sensed that she was slowly starting to accept him, narcissism and all.

◆

With the shade extermination behind her, Hana intended to enjoy her fill of the villa she had worked so hard for, and she leisurely strolled through its halls.

That said, once she'd made a circuit, she was left with a lot of free time and nothing to do with it.

The villa's western-style interior and exterior were refreshing, but in terms of manors, the Ichinomiya residence was still a cut above. Since Hana had grown used to living in the Ichinomiya house, the novelty of the villa wore off after the first hour.

Driven by boredom, Hana sought out Saku. "Heyyy, Saku," she said as she entered the room.

Saku was typing on his laptop. Even now, he was busy with work. "What?" he said.

"I'm borrred. Isn't there anything fun to do around here?"

He looked up from the screen. "You're really something." His gaze was equal parts amazed and weary. "Shouldn't you be overjoyed by your new villa?"

"I am, I am, but I thought about it. *Really* thought about it, and well, there's nothing to do," she admitted. "I'm bored. There's no TV here, and my phone's not getting any service, either."

"Can't be helped. There's a strong barrier around this entire area to prevent shades from escaping, and radio waves can't get through. There also aren't any TVs or radios since there's noise interference. That might be because of the shades, too."

"What about the laptop you're using?" Hana asked.

"It's not connected to the internet. I'm just drafting up documents for work."

The villa was literally a haunted house, and more so for the utter lack of entertainment.

Unfortunately, Hana wasn't some wise, old sage who had achieved enlightenment, so the lack of recreational activities was driving her up the wall.

"Nothing in the neighborhood, either?" she asked desperately.

"No, there are things to do nearby," Saku answered. "This area is filled with natural hot springs, so there's a popular *onsen* district close by. Plenty of shops, too, I believe."

"Say that sooner!" Hana chided. "Can I go out?"

"Wait a moment. I'll wrap this up and go with you."

"Aren't you busy?"

His hands had never stopped moving. He didn't seem like he had the time to be playing around.

"Not a problem. I thought the cleanup would take the entire day, so I kept my schedule free," he replied blithely.

Hana's eyes narrowed. He knew exactly how much work the property needed and still had the nerve to foist it on someone else.

Saku had attained the highest rank for practitioners, Obsidian rank. A task that took him a full day to do was no easy feat, and yet he had dumped the chore onto Hana as easily as if he was treating her to convenience-store ice cream. Should she take that as proof that he had faith in her ability? She honestly wasn't sure.

"I'm nearly done. Don't go anywhere," he said arrogantly before looking back to his screen.

Nothing for it. Hana obediently settled into a nearby sofa and passed the time joking around with Azuha.

Aoi wasn't around because he and Tsubaki were racing around the villa in a high-stakes game of tag. The two of them were on par with each other in terms of capability, so it wasn't easy for Aoi to give her the slip; he was running with all his might.

It would've been easier for him to hurry up and give in to the inevitable, but he seriously couldn't handle Tsubaki. Her feelings didn't seem like they'd be getting through to him anytime soon.

Was Aoi going to break first, or would Tsubaki find a new darling first? Secretly, Hana was eagerly watching their relationship play out, but she wasn't about to admit that to Aoi.

Besides Aoi, Miyabi and Arashi weren't in the room, either. The two had gone out on a walk in the garden and were lazily basking in the sunshine.

Hana was relieved that Arashi, the newbie in the shikigami gang, was getting along with everyone. He might have been a shikigami like the others, but he was also an actual deity. She had been worried he was going to let his pride take center stage, but he was subtly giving the three shikigami—his seniors—their due.

She wished she could take even a shred of Arashi's decency and stick it into a certain conceited lord. Maybe then he would learn to have some humility.

After loafing about for a while, she heard the *schnick* of the laptop being folded shut and looked at Saku. "Done?"

"Yeah."

"Let's get a move on, then!"

Tired of doing nothing but sitting and waiting, Hana sprang up from the couch and excitedly dashed out the room.

"You must've been bored out of your mind," commented Saku, following Hana out. His gaze was kind and soft as if he was looking at a mischievous child.

"What do we do about Aoi and the others? Call for them?" Hana asked.

"Leave them," Saku said. "They seem to be in the middle of a highly stimulating game of tag."

Tsubaki was no doubt having fun, but Aoi didn't seem to share the sentiment. Regardless, taking those two troublemakers along to a place packed with tourists was asking for complications, so Hana agreed to leave Aoi behind.

The servants pulled the car around. Hana and Saku, along with Azuha, got in and headed into town. Their destination was a five- to ten-minute drive from the overlook the villa stood on. They pulled into the *onsen* district. The scent of sulfur wafted through the air.

Since it wasn't a workday, the streets were crowded with people. The shops were doing good business, too; many had lines in front of them.

"I can't believe there's such a popular *onsen* area near the villa. The property's location is really top-notch. But just its location," Hana said.

"Isn't it? Have you taken a shine to it?"

"It'd be perfect if it wasn't infested with shades."

"It's perfect anyway as long as you're skilled enough to deal with the issue, don't you think? You have Arashi, and you're hardly lacking in combat ability yourself," Saku said. "But since it sits next to a busy district, make sure the shades don't get out, will you? There's a barrier around the property, but still—you never know what could happen."

"What a paaain," Hana complained.

If the shades escaped into this *onsen* area, a tourist destination, she would be the one held responsible. Not only had Saku dumped the villa on her, but he had other obligations for her, too. He had fobbed off a truly annoying problem onto her.

"The villa shades only need to be exterminated every six months or so. I've been busy with the succession and the inugami affair, so I haven't been able to check up on it. That's why there were so many shades this time. Normally, there are fewer. If you come more frequently, with your ability, it should be far from backbreaking work."

"I see. Well, it might work out, then."

Without the shade infestation, the villa was undeniably a superb property.

Hana fielded attacks from powerful shades on a regular basis, so getting rid of shades wasn't a difficult task for her. She'd only complained so much because of the excessive numbers. If there were only a few of them, Hana, with Arashi as one of her shikigami, would make quick work of them.

With that reasoning, the villa, with its oceanside view and nearby *onsen* town, just might be a good reward after all…or so she convinced herself. She had no other choice at this point.

"Master, let's look around. Hurry up," Azuha urged from her perch in Hana's hair. The shikigami had never gone out on a trip before. It was possible she was more excited than she was letting on.

"You're right. Let's go," Hana said.

She started to walk forward but was thrown off rhythm when Saku immediately grabbed her hand.

"Saku!" she cried out in surprise.

"We wouldn't want you to get lost, right?" He smirked, brimming with confidence. "Besides, this way, it'll be more like a date."

Hana, her face red, found herself unable to shake off his grip. In fact, quite the opposite, she lightly squeezed his hand back.

They wandered through the streets. Hana bought hot-spring eggs—a must-try when visiting an *onsen*—bit into steaming hot buns, and enjoyed a perfectly swirled soft serve.

Eventually, Saku ran out of patience and complained, "All you're doing is eating!"

"Well, everything looks so delicious," replied Hana.

"You're not going to have room for dinner," Saku warned like a mother cautioning a child.

However, his words went in one ear and out the next. Hana's attention was stolen away by the footbath that she had spotted.

"Look, Saku! They have a footbath here."

Hana pulled Saku forward by the hand. Saku shook his head in resignation, but his eyes were warm.

She bought a bottle of soda nearby before walking up to the footbath, taking off her shoes and socks, and dipping her feet in. "Come on, Saku." She patted the seat beside her, coaxing the reluctant Saku.

He gave in. After removing his shoes and socks, he rolled up his jeans and sunk his feet into the hot water.

"Mmm, the water feels amaaazing." Hana took a swig of her soda, looking nothing like the high school girl she was supposed to be. "Haaah," she sighed, "that hits the spot!"

"What are you, a middle-aged man?" Saku said.

"So what? Gotta enjoy myself while I'm here. It's my first time visiting an *onsen*," she said. "Does the villa get water from the springs, too?"

"Yeah, it's drawn straight from the source."

Straight from the source. How sweet those words sounded.

"Hooray! I'm taking a bath right after we get back."

"If you'd like, I'll scrub your back myself," Saku offered with a quirk of his lips.

Hana narrowed her eyes. "Perverted old man," she accused.

"No need to be shy—we're married."

"There is *so* a need!"

"I suppose bathing together might be too high of a hurdle for you, considering you never even kissed anyone before me. It'll have to wait until you gain a bit more experience."

Blushing furiously, Hana concentrated her energy into her palm and threw it at Saku. It dispersed when it hit him, but he still looked extremely flustered.

"Hey, watch it!" he exclaimed. "What do you think you're doing in public?"

Normal people—people who weren't practitioners, that was—couldn't see concentrated balls of energy. However, Hana was powerful enough that she could send people flying with such an attack, like she had done to Saku's younger brother, Nozomu, in the past.

Saku was skilled himself, which was why the attack had fizzled, but it would've badly hurt a normal person.

Of course, Hana had thought things through properly before she had acted. "It's your fault, Saku! Besides, I restrained myself."

In reality, the attack hurt less than a flick to the forehead.

"If this is all it takes to embarrass you, where are we supposed to go from here? The couples of the world do much more extreme things all the time, you know," Saku said.

What garbage is this man saying with such a serious face?

"I'll divorce you before it comes to that!" Hana barked.

He looked at her with amusement. Then he snickered, his shoulders quaking with laughter.

That was when she realized he was only trying to get a rise out of her.

"Aw, come on," Hana said. "You should fix that personality of yours. I'm serious. Your popularity is going to plummet."

"Don't worry. Not a problem. I only have eyes for you, Hana," he declared without a trace of embarrassment.

She was at a loss for how to respond. "That's exactly what I'm talking about! Stop playing with me!"

"I'm serious," he said. "You're not going to understand unless I tell you straight, right? I'm just being honest with my expressions of affection."

"Stop it already. There are people around," she protested.

Two middle-aged women sat across from them, enjoying the footbath and tittering to each other. Were those smirks on their faces Hana was seeing?

"It sure is nice to be young."

"I remember being that age, too."

Their conversation was perfectly audible from where Hana and Saku were sitting, and their words stabbed straight at her sense of embarrassment. Her heart wasn't going to be able to take it if they stayed here any longer.

Hana drew her feet out of the bath and was about to dry them off, when Saku snatched the towel from her hands and began to carefully wipe her feet dry.

"Saku, wha—?!" she cried.

The pair of aunties grinned, exclaiming happily, ""My, oh my.""

Her urge to run doubled.

Saku paid no attention to her agitation and casually fended off her attempts to take back the towel. He thoroughly wiped up every water drop from her skin before he toweled his own feet off.

Completely mortified, Hana put her shoes and socks back on without a word and dashed away from the footbath.

"Hey, Hana! Wait up," Saku called.

"Not a chance!" she replied, her mood dark.

Does that man have no sense of shame? she wondered.

Indeed, Saku showed no hints of remorse. On the contrary, there seemed to be a new pep in his step.

It was no wonder seeing his face only pissed Hana off. "What are you smiling about?"

He snickered. "Heh-heh-heh. I'll never get tired of you, Hana."

"I don't get what you mean."

"I do. That's all that matters."

Was it Tsubaki who'd told Hana that Saku never used to smile?

She'd heard it said that Saku's facial muscles were dead, that he was as expressionless as a wax figure. Seeing the man by her side and his rich array of expressions, she could hardly believe it.

The laughing Saku was a hundred times more attractive than the stone-faced one, not that she'd ever admit it out loud.

She didn't protest when Saku took her hand again.

The two leisurely strolled the streets until they came to a shop selling *magatama* beads, small stone charms shaped like a comma. The sign claimed they were stones of power. The charms arranged on the display were made from a variety of stones.

"Do you want one?" Saku asked.

"Hmmm, let me think…," she said, reading the labels with the names of the stones along with the intended meaning and effects.

A white-agate bead caught her eye. She checked what it was supposed to do and smirked.

"You've got an evil look on your face," Saku remarked.

But Hana's expression didn't change. In fact, her grin only seemed to grow wider.

"Saku, I'm going to buy this white-agate *magatama* for you. It's a present from me to you, so be sure to wear it with your practitioner pendant," she told him. "Aren't you happy to be getting a present from your beloved wife?"

Saku wasn't foolish enough to swallow Hana's story so easily, not with that smirk on her face. He looked at her suspiciously, then said, "Fine, but what are you planning?"

"How rude. It's my thanks for the lovely villa you gave me," she said, taking not just one, but two of the stones to the register, a spring in her step. "Heh-heh." She bought them and handed one to Saku. "Here ya go. Put it on."

"Fine."

He slipped the *magatama* stone onto the same chain where he wore the obsidian pendant—the pendants stood as practitioner licenses—all the while wondering why in the world she had bought two.

The stone was small and didn't pose a nuisance. It dangled around Saku's neck, nestled next to his practitioner pendant.

"What are you going to do with the other one?" he asked.

"Rainy-day insurance."

Hana's answer didn't clear anything up, but seeing how lively she was, Saku didn't push the matter further.

After that, they explored the town more, bought a mountain of souvenirs, and returned to the villa triumphantly.

Aoi was waiting for them, dragging along Tsubaki, who was glued tightly to him. He was nearly in tears. "How could you leave me here?" he whined. "Where did you go?"

"I got to spend a whole day with my darling! I'm in bliss," Tsubaki said.

"Get her offa me already," he pleaded.

Hana and Saku exchanged a look and sighed deeply. Neither had imagined the shikigamis' game of tag would continue for so long after the two of them had left for the *onsen*.

Chapter 2

After returning to the Ichinomiyas' main residence, Hana went straight to her room and collapsed onto a couch.

"Ahhh, I'm exhausted," she sighed.

The Ichinomiya residence had futons laid directly on tatami mats. However, the villa had western-style beds with mattresses.

When Hana had dived onto the bed, the springy mattress had folded her into its embrace. She fondly remembered how comfortable the mattress had been. It was high quality, as far as Hana could tell, and had the power to whisk the weary traveler straight into the world of sleep.

Should she ask for a bed to be put in her room at the Ichinomiya residence, too? That way, she'd be able to fall straight asleep whenever she wanted to get some rest.

Those were the thoughts going through her head when Saku barged into the room without even knocking.

He saw Hana sprawled out limply on the couch and said, "You're slacking off."

"Well, sure. I was forced onto shade-extermination duty right after arriving at the villa. What did you expect? This is all your fault," Hana shot back. "On top of that, this morning, the shades that were *supposed to have been eradicated* came welling out of the brickwork, and I had to deal with them all by myself. I was counting on you to lend me a hand only to find out you'd left Tsubaki and gone home first."

Hana had been stunned when Tsubaki told her after she woke up that Saku was already gone. Then she'd looked outside to find the shades that she'd cleared out the day before prowling about the grounds again. A potentially pleasant morning, ruined.

"Plus," she continued, "Aoi was too busy running away from Tsubaki to be of any help. Didn't you say the grounds only need to be cleaned up occasionally? There were a ton of them this morning." She turned an accusatory glare on Saku from where she was lying on the couch.

"That was my bad. I was called back to deal with an emergency and didn't have time to tell you in person," Saku said. "But the shades you fought today were likely ones in the area drawn to your presence. They were unrelated to the villa's location, I believe."

The barrier around the property allowed shades in but not out. It acted like a trap. The villa was a magnet for shades, and Hana was targeted by shades on a regular basis. Add the two together, and what you got was an infestation. Saku hadn't anticipated that outcome.

"I got a report that the shades stopped appearing the moment you left, so there's no problem. Go and clear it out again when you have some time."

"Sure, sure."

Hana once again regretted taking on something so troublesome, but Saku was unlikely to agree to a return even if she demanded one now.

"You won't catch me believing a word you say next time," she warned.

"Don't be like that," replied Saku. "I'm counting on you."

Hana wanted nothing more than to wash her hands of the matter, but she had no choice. She sighed. "Ahhh, Arashi, comfort me."

She rose from the sofa, picked up Arashi from where he was lounging around nearby, and buried her face in his fluffy fur. The enchanting pillowy softness pieced together her fragmented heart.

The shikigami seemed exasperated, but he let Hana do as she liked without struggling.

What a benevolent god he was. Granted, his big heart was precisely the reason he had ended up as a tatarigami, a cursed spirit.

"By the way, what was the emergency?" Hana asked. "Is that why the atmosphere here has been so strained since I got back?"

"So you noticed."

"Of course. Anyone would, whether they wanted to or not. You could cut the tension with a knife."

The Ichinomiya residence had been swarming with grave-faced practitioners from the Association.

Since it was the residence of the main family, practitioners with their license pendants around their necks regularly came and went, but the traffic was heavier than usual. Even an idiot would realize something was different.

Saku sat down cross-legged facing Hana, who held Arashi in her arms. His face was grim as he said, "The Association of Practitioners' headquarters was broken into."

"Are you serious?" Hana said.

"Yeah. The culprits escaped. The investigation is underway."

"Oof."

Hana looked aghast, as anyone would be. She had intended to find employment at a regular company, so she hadn't bothered to learn about the Association of Practitioners in depth, but even she had heard about the strict security at the headquarters.

The facility was proud of its security, which kept all outsiders *out*. Not a single ant was allowed past its walls.

It was astonishing enough that someone had thought to *try* to break in, let alone actually go through with the act. On top of that, they had gotten away.

"Isn't the Association's security good?" Hana asked.

"Airtight," answered Saku, "but it appears whoever did it had eyes and ears on the inside. After the incident, several practitioners went off the grid."

"My condolences. What else can I say? That's grave news."

"You're telling me," he said with a deep sigh, radiating irritation.

"The intruders… They didn't break in just for the fun of it, did they?"

Had that been the case, there wouldn't have been a need to mobilize so many practitioners, she surmised.

Her guess was spot-on.

"Yeah, they stole a few talismans that were being held in the building," Saku replied.

"Ones made by the Nijouin clan?"

"Unfortunately, yes. Not to mention, each and every one was SS rank in terms of the risk they pose."

"That's horrible!" Hana cried.

"Now you know why everyone's on edge."

He sent a withering look her way, which seemed to say, *Come on, keep up.* That hurt.

Even Hana knew how nasty the higher-ranking talismans were supposed to be.

Spelled talismans got a bad rep, but in fact, not all of them were dangerous to humans.

Most of them had been created to fight shades. They could be considered magical shade-killing weapons.

However, the SS-rank talismans, if used for evil, had the potential to cause massive destruction and damage to humans as well, which was why they had been sealed away.

As the daughter of a branch family with low political influence, Hana knew nothing about what effects the talismans might have. However, she had learned in class that the Association handled the deadliest of talismans. That, and the fact that all SS-rank talismans had been created by the Nijouin clan.

"How could something so dangerous be so easily stolen?" Hana demanded. "Isn't the headquarters under the Ichinomiyas' jurisdiction? In other words, you're the one who's most responsible!" She pointed an accusatory—not to mention rude—finger at Saku.

"Why do you think I'm so stressed out?!" he shouted back, his eyes wide.

Hana suspected that he was venting his frustration on her, but considering the predicament he was in, she let it go.

Saku's hands flew to his head. "You can count the number of major incidents since the Association's establishment on one hand. How could this have happened in my generation…? I can already hear that old fool's mocking laughter if he hears about this." He looked seriously worried.

Hana figured he was referring to his father. She'd heard him speak of the former clan lord derogatorily on occasion.

She had yet to meet the man, and the relationship between the father and son was still a mystery to her.

Saku had said they weren't on good terms before, and whenever Hana broached the subject of Saku's father at the dinner table, the vibe in the room would darken. She'd learned not to ask.

She'd heard from Towa, a veteran member of the staff and the only one who got away with calling Saku "Junior," that he was well, so she figured she would have the chance to meet him eventually.

But enough about Saku's father. The problem at hand was the thieves who'd broken into the Association's headquarters.

"Do you think you can find them?" Hana asked.

"Everyone who can be spared is working on the investigation. Some troublesome types seem to be involved, so the other clans are lending a hand as well."

"Troublesome types?" she echoed.

"The Skull and Spider Lily are making their move."

"Th-the skull and what now?" Hana tilted her head quizzically. The question *What in the world are you talking about?* was scrawled plainly across her face.

Saku covered his eyes with one hand. "You were born into a branch family of one of the five clans... How can you not know?"

He looked like he was at the end of his rope, like he was accusing Hana of...of some sort of crime. It ticked Hana off. "I don't know what I don't know. 'The Skull and Spider Lily,' was it? So? What of it?"

"A button embossed with a skull and spider lily was found at the scene of the crime. It's known to be the mark of a long-running terrorist organization. They're commonly called the Skull of Nirvana." The spider lily is a symbol of the Buddhist holiday Higan, when people pay respect to their ancestors.

"That's a leap," she said, snickering.

Saku karate-chopped her on the head to shut her up before continuing, "The Skull of Nirvana consists of lowlifes intent on taking down the five clans, who have great influence within the country because of our task to protect the pillars. Their excuse is that they want to free the country from the clans' domination."

"A straightforward ideology for a terrorist group," Hana said. "So they know about the pillars. Does that mean they're all from practitioner families?"

"Exactly. It's a gathering of practitioners who have been, for whatever reason, belittled or ignored. None of them are particularly talented, either, so we've mostly left the organization alone. However, recently, they've suddenly grown more powerful and have been causing all sorts of trouble. Their crimes can no longer be overlooked. The five clans were right on the verge of giving an official directive for practitioners to watch their backs and work toward dismantling the group."

"Oh, I see," Hana said disinterestedly like it was none of her business.

"These are people who disdain the five clans for their influence. They're watching and waiting for a crack in our defenses to bring the clans down. The clans are their enemy. That means there's a chance they would target the wife of the Ichinomiya lord, too. That's you, Hana."

"Wha—?!" Hana gaped at Saku. She had been so optimistic the terrorists would have nothing to do with her. "You're kidding, right?!"

"Regrettably, no. They stole dangerous talismans. There's no guarantee they aren't planning on doing something extreme with them."

She glared at him. "This is a disaster!"

"That's what I've been trying to tell you, idiot!" He flicked her hard on the forehead.

"Ow! What are you doing?!"

"You aren't listening to me."

"What do you expect?" Hana protested. "I may be an Obsidian High student, but I've always been stuck in Class C. I was going to live my life as a regular person. I had no interest in anything having to do with practitioners and no interest in my studies."

"You're the wife of the clan lord. Take an interest," he said dryly.

Saku's speech did not—surprise, surprise—suddenly inspire Hana to study.

She'd divorce him eventually, get her compensation, and live out the rest of her life carefree.

There was no reason for her to remember all the nitty-gritty details about the practitioners' world.

Saku, who had likely guessed exactly what Hana was thinking, smiled wickedly. "If you don't show any improvement, I'll have no choice but to ask my mother to tutor you."

A hideous threat, if there ever was one.

Hana's expression grew pinched. "Anything but that!"

Not only did Mio have a tsundere personality, but one could also tell just by looking at her that she would be very strict when it came to her daughter-in-law's education. Maybe she was even a perfectionist?

Hana wouldn't last a day studying under Mio's direct tutelage, no question about it.

Mio was strict with both other people and herself, whereas Hana was strict with others but soft on herself. The two of them mixed like oil and water.

War was sure to break out between the new bride and the mother-in-law.

"Hurry up and get up to speed, then," Saku said unsympathetically.

Hana's face scrunched in distaste. "Whaaat? We're gonna get divorced soon anyway, so what's it matter?"

Saku's eye twitched. His face was drawn tight, but he nevertheless forced his lips into a smile before going on the offense. "I see, I see," he said. "You're really dead set on divorcing me... In that case, shall I give you a reason to stay?" He took Hana's hand, drew her close, and pushed her down onto the tatami mats.

Hana froze. Now that she was confronted with Saku's handsome face a breath away from hers, all thoughts of fleeing went straight out the window.

Arashi calmly cut in. "It is not becoming of a man to resort to force."

"Be quiet. Humans have complex emotions a god couldn't hope to understand!" Saku retorted.

"Hmm, oh? Is that so? But Hana's turned into a statue from shock. Are you all right with that?"

"More than all right. This is perfect. She runs when approached with tact. Force is the only way."

"You should treat women with care."

"This is a problem between husband and wife. Stay out of it."

Hovering over Hana on all fours, Saku continued to duke it out with Arashi. He didn't notice Hana quietly shaking with rage.

"I'll show you 'force is the only way'! Dirty old man!" she yelled, driving a fist into Saku's stomach from where she lay prone beneath him.

"Guh—!"

The beautiful right hook left him groaning in pain and clutching his stomach. She followed the hook with a kick that sent him sprawling.

She lifted Arashi into her arms. "Arashi, words are useless at times like this. You have to send him flying like Aoi does," she instructed. "Don't just watch, okay? Stop him."

"Oh, really? I wasn't sure if it was okay for me to stick my nose into a couple's problem…," the shikigami said.

"Perfectly okay, so next time, help me immediately!" she urged, her expression intent.

"Understood." Contrary to his words, he still seemed perplexed, but he nodded.

In the meantime, Saku had finally recovered enough to move, albeit jerkily; he was still in pain. "Do you mean to kill me, Hana?!"

"You get what you deserve!"

"You were the one who brought up divorce. I only thought a baby would put an end to any such thoughts, no?"

"That would be all the more reason to split up!! You better be prepared to pay for a marital settlement agreement. I'll wring you dry!"

Towa's voice from outside Hana's room interrupted their arguing. "Oh-hoh-hoh-hoh, hearing the two of you get along makes this old woman terribly happy." She then announced, "Junior, you have a guest."

Apparently, it was time for Saku to get to work.

With an exasperated expression and an arm wrapped around his middle, he climbed to his feet. "Stop it with the 'Junior' already, Towa."

She laughed and proceeded to immediately ignore his order. "Hoh-hoh-hoh. As you say, Junior."

His expression became crestfallen. He warned her off every time, but Towa was someone he was unable to strong-arm. He seemed resigned.

Towa had been working for the Ichinomiyas since before Saku was born. Indeed, under this roof, she may have been the most powerful one of all.

Even the prickly and stern Mio treated Towa, and Towa alone, with a level of formal courtesy. It was clear that she acknowledged the older servant's position.

On his way out of Hana's room, Saku paused and looked back. "Like I said earlier, watch out for the Skull of Nirvana. Make sure you take the car to and from school."

"'Kaaay. I'll keep an eye out," she said, "not that I'd know what a terrorist would look like."

"That can't be helped. But don't go following anyone suspicious."

"You don't have to worry about that. I'm not a child."

What are you, my mother? The complaint flashed through Hana's mind, the way he was fussing over her. She looked at him with a fed up expression.

"I'll be busy for the time being. If you need anything, ask my mother," Saku told her.

"Got it."

His lips quirked into a smile. "Be a good girl." He ruffled her hair and left the room.

◆

As Saku predicted, he became inundated with work and spent his days rushing in and out of the residence. He was busy to the point that he was absent from family meals, leaving the seat for the clan lord empty.

"Is Saku out on business again today?" Hana asked Towa.

"It appears so," the servant answered with an apologetic expression, though she wasn't to blame.

"They haven't been recovered yet...?" Hana mumbled to herself, speaking of the talismans stolen from the headquarters. If the clans were to take them back, they had to do so quickly.

"Miss Hana, you are not registered with the Association and are a student no less. This matter has nothing to do with you," Saku's mother said. "You must conduct yourself properly as the mistress of the clan."

Mio's tone was harsh, making the listener feel as if they were being scolded, and her almond-shaped eyes always seemed reproachful. At first, Hana had felt intimidated by Mio's severe countenance, but recently, she'd caught glimpses of the matriarch's hidden soft side.

Even now, her words, which sounded censorious, were actually meant to comfort. She was reassuring Hana not to worry. What an inscrutable way to show she cared.

Hana couldn't help but think that Mio's severe tone and glaring eyes must cost her greatly.

Fortunately, the servants in the residence were all familiar with their mistress's complex personality.

Hana instinctively sat up straighter, as she always did when speaking with Mio. "Y-yes, ma'am!"

"Good. Then let us eat."

Satisfied with Hana's answer, Mio picked up her chopsticks. Hana and Nozomu, who had been watching quietly from the side, picked up theirs as well, and they dug in.

The three quickly finished their breakfast. It was time for Hana and Nozomu to head to school.

"Nozomuuu. Why not come with your big sis to school once in a while?" Hana teased.

"Why would I, stupid?! Don't think you have my approval!" Nozomu shouted, his face bright red. He got into his designated car, and it drove off right away.

Hana saw him off with a grin on her face. If Saku had been here, he would have told her to stop teasing Nozomu.

It had been a while since she had first come to live with the Ichinomiyas, but even now, she and Nozomu never spoke beyond the bare minimum of conversation.

Yet she had stumbled upon the knowledge that Nozomu was harboring a secret brother complex. He tended to lash out despite his love and admiration for Saku, and she couldn't resist needling the prickly boy. He avoided her like the plague as a result, but she continued to approach him without paying his attitude any mind.

Nozomu himself hadn't realized she knew his secret, which was highly amusing to Hana. She was keeping an eagle eye out for the perfect opportunity to reveal the ace up her sleeve.

"When should I put the *magatama* to use?" she mused cheerfully as she got into her own car.

At school, Hana was still dismissed as a waste of space. Since she had displayed her powers before the Ichinomiya household, the family and staff were aware of her true abilities. However, off the premises, her reputation did a one-eighty.

She had once thoroughly thrashed Nozomu, too, but that little tidbit had not made the rounds at Obsidian High.

As the second son of the Ichinomiya head family, he was no doubt embarrassed that he had been powerless to raise a finger against Hana, a daughter of a mere branch family, all the more because she was known as her older sister's scraps to everyone else.

Hana neither blamed him—she was familiar with the Class A students' overinflated sense of pride—nor had any intention of spreading the story of her victory herself.

She hoped that she would be able to continue passing as good-for-nothing, but cracks were starting to appear in her charade.

The cause was Saku. Ever since they'd gotten married, he'd been drawing on her abilities. The inugami incident and the extermination of the villa were only the beginning. He was sure to demand more of her from now on, and the more she helped Saku, the higher the risk of her true power being leaked to the world.

Once her secret was out, she would have no choice but to give up. She had decided she would leave the fallout and headaches to Saku. In the meantime, she attended classes as usual.

At present, Hana was in class listening to a lecture, and she was bored out of her mind. She hid a yawn behind her textbook.

She had never felt the slightest desire to become a practitioner, so there was no reason for her to attend Obsidian High.

Since Saku had told her to study up, she was awake, which was in and of itself unusual, but there was just no fending off the drowsiness that was battering her in waves.

Give up. Take a nap, whispered the devil on her shoulder.

She told herself she could try again the next day and was just about to slip into dreamland when a loud *boom* sounded from the school yard.

The shock wave from the thunderous crash shook the windows and slapped Hana awake.

The students buzzed with curiosity and immediately proceeded to ignore class in favor of swarming the windows.

"Was that an explosion?"

"Did something happen?"

"Doesn't Class A have its practical now?"

The mention of Class A snagged Hana's attention. She broke through the crowd of gawkers and looked out the window to see the Class A third-years in the middle of class. Instinctively, she scanned the crowd for Hazuki.

In addition to the students, the grounds were packed with shikigami. Had they been dueling with their shikigami, maybe? Hana was having trouble locating Hazuki in the pack...

"There! I found your sister, Hana!" her best friend, Suzu, exclaimed. She had come up next to Hana while Hana had been distracted.

Hana looked toward where Suzu was pointing. Next to a crater, where the explosion had likely originated, stood Hazuki.

Hana saw Nozomu rush to her sister's side, his face pale, but the other students kept their distance.

What in the world had happened? Hana couldn't tell from where she was standing.

"Azuha, can you erase your presence and go investigate for me?" she asked.

Since she was surrounded by classmates, Azuha didn't reply but simply vanished silently.

Their teacher clapped loudly to get everyone's attention. "All right, calm down and return to your seats!"

Everyone was still curious, of course, but it seemed like the practical was over for the day. Outside in the school yard, the Class A students were recalling their shikigami, so the Class C students peeled away from the windows and sat back down.

Nevertheless, their thoughts were still preoccupied by the incident, and no one could focus for the rest of class.

Azuha returned during the break between classes. Since Hana didn't want the fact that Azuha could speak to be known, she decided to ditch her next class.

Hana holed up in an empty classroom and put up a barrier to prevent others from entering.

"What did you find out?" she asked Azuha.

"Your older sister lost control of her power, it seems," the shikigami answered.

"Hazuki did?"

Hana was surprised. While Hazuki was powerful enough to manifest a human shikigami, Hana had never heard of her sister's power running rampant.

Hazuki had always been skilled at modulating her power. Even as a young child, she had kept a tight rein on herself.

Hana had a hard time believing that Hazuki, of all people, would let her power get away from her at this age.

"Does that mean that something shook her so badly that she couldn't keep control?" Hana muttered.

All practitioners knew that one's emotional state of mind had a great impact on one's powers. That was why it was the first explanation to come to mind.

However, since Hana had left the Ichise house, there was no way for her to know what had been going on around Hazuki recently.

"Does it bother you, Master?" asked Azuha bluntly.

Hana's face scrunched as if she'd just bitten into something bitter. "You could say that…"

She thought she had broken off all ties to her family when she left the house, and yet she couldn't help but worry about Hazuki.

If this had been an incident involving her parents, she would have easily dismissed it with a simple *Oh, I see*, but this was Hazuki. She could tell herself to turn a blind eye all she wanted, but she was still curious in spite of herself. Was that because they were twins?

But Hana thought that even if she were to stick her nose in at this point, Hazuki would only demand to know why she was interfering and would drive her away.

Hana was no longer permitted to care about Hazuki. Hana had made sure of that herself.

"What should I do…?"

Their older brother, Yanagi, might know.

However, it had been a long time since she'd stopped talking to Yanagi. Needless to say, she didn't even know his number.

Even if she could call him, what would she say?

Then again, Yanagi hardly ever went home, so Hana didn't truly believe he would know about Hazuki's situation.

They might have been siblings, but their relationship was paper-thin. There might not be anything she could say that would be of any use.

"Aghhh, I don't know," Hana groaned.

She was sure that the Ichise family was the reason why Hazuki had been shaken enough for her to lose control of her powers. Their parents, who considered their children nothing more than tools, had probably made an impossible demand of her.

Hana had run away, unable to put up with those parents any longer.

Whenever she thought about the fact that Hazuki was still living inside the cage that their parents had built, she was struck by an unnameable emotion.

"She's...not supposed to mean anything to me..."

Hana covered her eyes with both hands, all the better to hide the emotions she thought she'd thrown away long ago that had come welling up to the surface.

Just what was she supposed to do?

She had no answers. A wave of helplessness swept through her and immobilized her.

◆

The school day ended with Hana still at a loss for what to do. On top of that, she'd forgotten Saku's warning to keep her guard up, and she took a detour on the way home for a change of pace.

Farther along was a café that served a parfait she liked.

Her face might have been scrunched in concentration, but her head was filled with thoughts of the dessert.

"Parfait, yummy, yummy. Get in my hungry tummy," she chanted in a singsong voice, making the lyrics up as she walked.

Her singing was interrupted by someone calling to her out of the blue. "Um, you're Miss Hana Ichise, correct?"

The cute voice stopped her in her tracks. Hana turned around to find a twitchy and nervous girl around her age staring at her intently. Her chestnut hair was cut in a bob and styled in loose waves. Her downturned eyes gave her a perpetual puppy face; the effect was endearing and engendered an urge to protect the girl.

Next to her stood an athletic young man with matching features and close-cropped black hair. He was slightly taller than Nozomu.

Hana startled at the sight of them and backed away. There was nothing special about the pair, but looming behind them were men in suits with death glares who resembled the fierce Nio Buddhist guardians.

Hana knew from a single glance she should not get involved with these people, so she turned on her heel and dashed away.

The girl panicked and shouted at Hana's fleeing back. "W-wait! Please!!"

No one was foolish enough to dutifully obey such a plea. The girl's words only inspired Hana to run faster. The Nio guardians came swarming after her, too. Terrifying.

Unfortunately, the boy caught her easily. When she shook off his hand, he let go without a fight.

When the girl finally caught up, she huffed, "Geez! Why did you run?" Her eyes were shiny with tears of frustration.

"Who wouldn't run in this situation?" Hana demanded. Didn't the girl see the gods of wrath behind her? When confronted with such menacing pressure, anyone would choose flight.

The girl caught her breath. She still seemed rather nervous, but her voice was firm when she said, "We have business with you. Come with us."

"No can do." Hana's refusal followed hot on the trail of the girl's demand. "I was given a stern warning against following suspicious individuals."

"We are not suspicious!" the girl protested, her voice shaking with outrage.

"That's what all suspicious people say."

"We're not!"

Hana was struck by déjà vu—hadn't she had this conversation before?

She made to push past, but the boy grabbed her wrist again. She glared at him wordlessly. He stared back at her without saying a word. His expression didn't change a single bit.

While the two of them were locked in a stare down, the girl waved one of the men in black forward and snatched off the pendant hanging around his neck.

Hana was shocked to see it was something she recognized, something she was actually quite familiar with. "That's…the pendant of the Association of Practitioners."

The others bent to reveal their pendants to Hana as well. The pendants were all white or gold, no exception, which meant they were all First or Second Color practitioners, even though they had the intimidating presence of Obsidian ranks as far as looks went. How anticlimactic.

But as far as proof of identity went, the pendants more than served their purpose.

The girl said, "Are you going to listen now?"

"For now. But don't misunderstand. I don't trust you," Hana said. "You've heard about the intruders who broke into the Association, right? The culprits were practitioners, apparently."

"W-we didn't do it!"

"So prove it."

Hana had Azuha stand by so that she could flee the moment the pair did anything suspicious.

The girl was flummoxed by Hana's tight guard and mistrust, and tears came to her eyes. "Proof…proof…er, um," she stuttered. Finally, she sought help from the boy who was holding Hana's wrist captive. "Kiriya, what do we do?"

Kiriya took his phone from his pocket and showed Hana the screen, which displayed a picture of Saku; smiling next to him was the girl standing in front of her.

Hana's eyes widened. "You're Saku's friends?"

The boy then opened his mouth for the first time. "We're the grand-children of the head of the Nijouin clan. I'm Kiriya. That's Kikiyo. It's a pleasure to meet you." He bowed politely, though he remained poker-faced.

Hana was dumbfounded. In a trance, she bowed back. "And I, you. Thank you for your courtesy." As she straightened up, she suddenly pieced together what he had said. "Wait, grandchildren? Of Nijouin?"

"Yeah, that's right," he replied.

"Oh, I see… Ah-ha-ha-ha…" She had to laugh. If Saku found out that she had called the direct descendants of the Nijouin bloodline *suspicious*, he would tear her new one.

"There's your proof, all right? *Now* will you come with us?" asked Kikiyo. She was so timid, Hana wanted to ask what she was so scared of.

If they were from the Nijouin clan, there was no reason for her to refuse. Hana nodded. Azuha had been standing ready to use her power whenever Hana signaled. Hana relieved her from watch duty.

Hana decided she could listen to whatever they had to say at the café she'd originally been planning to go to. There, she ordered the store's most popular parfait. The waitstaff brought water for them after taking their order.

The seats around Hana, Kikiyo, and Kiriya were completely filled by the Nio guardian wannabes.

What a surreal sight.

The café was a popular one, but there were few customers at the moment. The men in black were no doubt the reason. They packed the window seats, visible from outside, and frightened pedestrians on the streets.

Hana worried they were going to be yelled at for harming the shop's business.

She took a sip of her drink, sighed, and broached the discussion herself. "So? What did you want to talk to me about?"

She looked at Kikiyo and Kiriya in turn, but Kiriya seemed to be waiting for Kikiyo to speak. The one who had business with Hana was her.

"...reak...miya," Kikiyo mumbled in a barely audible voice.

"Say again?" Hana said.

"Please break up with Lord Ichinomiya!"

Hana gaped. "What?"

Kikiyo pressed on with no regard for Hana's shock. "Lord Ichinomiya is an exceptional person! He's the youngest practitioner ever to obtain the Obsidian rank, he became the clan lord at such an early age, *and* he successfully restored the barrier around the pillar without any issues. He's a brilliant practitioner and a brilliant man. Yet the one who became his wife was a—a...good-for-nothing like you."

She peeked at Hana as she spoke as if she was checking to see if Hana was angry at her. "I would be able to bear your twin sister being chosen, but compared with you, I'd definitely be more helpful to Lord Ichinomiya!"

"In short," Hana said, "you're in love with Saku, and you want to be his wife."

Kikiyo looked down at the table, her cheeks bright red. "Th-th-that's— I don't..."

After that caustic speech, she was picking *now* to get shy?

"Well, I'll think about it," Hana said.

The girl's face instantly lit up. "Wha—? Really?!"

But as much as she'd like to, Hana couldn't just wrap up the conversation with *Yes, of course*. Instead, she said, "Yeah, but..."

"What is it?"

"...I've cut off ties to the Ichises, you see. Saku is lending me his support with various things, and I've asked for his help finding a job, too,"

Hana explained. "If I part ways with him, I'd have to start again from zero and somehow eke out a living by myself."

They were going to get divorced regardless, but it probably wouldn't be anytime soon.

That was to say, Saku was strangely fixated on her at present, so until he lost interest, divorce was off the table.

At the end of the day, what Hana said didn't matter. Saku was the lord of the Ichinomiya clan. There was a world of difference between the authority they had.

"So I'm not sure I can divorce him," Hana concluded with a rueful smile, intending that to be the end of the matter.

However, Kikiyo gently slid a signed, blank check and pre-filled divorce papers to Hana. While Hana was stunned, Kikiyo said, "I will give you one billion yen if you leave Lord Ichinomiya."

"..." Hana was dumbfounded by the obscene amount of money and didn't reply.

Kikiyo apparently took her speechlessness as a refusal and raised the stakes. "One point five billion."

When Hana still didn't say a word, Kikiyo took things to the extreme. "Three billion!"

Cha-ching! rang the cash register in Hana's head. "Where do I sign?" she asked, cheerfully pulling a pen out of her bag and reaching for the papers.

Kikiyo perked up. "I did it, Kiriya."

He patted her on the head expressionlessly. "Good job. You did well." Despite his monotone voice and stony expression, neither of which had changed the entire time, he seemed to get along well with Kikiyo.

They're completely different from my family, Hana thought. However, the thought was quickly overshadowed by the prospect of the preposterous amount of money she was about to receive.

"So here? I sign here?" Hana asked again.

"Yes, that's right!" Kikiyo said.

"Will you really give me three billion yen? This isn't a scam?"

"Of course I will! The reputation of the Nijouin clan is on the line. I'll be sure to compensate you properly, so you have to do your part, too, and sign."

"I am, I am. I will happily sign whatever you want me to."

Hana touched her pen to the paper, her mood chipper.

"'Happily,' my butt, you idiot!"

The unexpected vitriol was accompanied by the whistle of a hand flying through the air. The chop to the back of her head launched her forward, and she only narrowly managed to avoid hitting her forehead on the table.

Who had the audacity to hit another person on the head without reservation? What hole did they crawl out from? Hana turned around to find Saku standing behind her, a vein throbbing on his temple.

"Crap, Saku," she cursed.

Saku goggled at her. "What do you mean, 'crap'?!" he demanded. "The bodyguards I assigned to you told me you were in the clutches of some punks from the main Nijouin family, and I dropped everything to check on you..."

He snatched the divorce papers out from under her hand and tore them into tiny pieces.

"Nooo. My three billion yeeen!" whined Hana.

"You money-grubber. Don't let money blind you so easily." He smacked her lightly on the head again. "What do you think you're doing?! I told you to take the car to and from school! You ignored *all* my instructions and ran off with strangers without a second thought! Didn't anyone tell you not to take candy from strangers?"

"You don't have to shout into my ear! I can hear you!" she snapped.

"Besides, can you blame me? It's three billion. *Billion!* I had to take the gamble even if I was being tricked!"

"Don't gamble, you giant moron! Normal people would know to turn down such a fishy offer." Saku tore up the check on the table.

Hana let out a wail of anguish. "My three billion!"

"It's not yours. Give it up," Saku said harshly. Then he switched targets and turned a glare toward her companions across the table. "...What's the deal, Kikiyo, Kiriya?"

Kikiyo paled, trembling with tension. "Ah, um, Lord Ichinomiya..."

Kiriya looked back at Saku without reacting.

"I don't know what kind of propaganda you're feeding her, but I have zero intention of divorcing Hana."

A hurt expression rose to Kikiyo's face at Saku's blunt rejection. Saku paid her no attention and continued, "This marriage is an issue—a *private* issue—for the Ichinomiyas. People from Nijouin have no say in the matter. If you pester Hana again, I'll have no choice but to take my complaints to the head of your clan, one clan lord to another, you know?"

"Eek, not Grandfather!" Kikiyo shrieked, shaken by Saku's threat.

"..." Kiriya didn't respond, but his expression changed for the first time, twisting in distaste.

While Hana was marveling at the visible sign of emotion, Saku grabbed her hand and pulled her with him toward the exit. Just as they were leaving, a waitress came around with the parfait she'd ordered. Hana dug in her heels but was inexorably dragged out. "Saku, wait. My parfait!" she whined.

"Forget it."

"I don't wanna."

But her resistance was useless. Saku dragged her out of the café with him and threw her into the car parked out front. She banged herself in various places on the way in. Her body ached from the landing.

"You're too rough. Can't you be any gentler?" she complained.

The corner of Saku's mouth twitched. "Who's the one causing trouble when I'm swamped as it is? Why don't you try acting like an adult?"

"You're being unreasonable. I was just going along, minding my own business and looking forward to my parfait, when *they* came looking for me."

"Is that right? You seemed pretty chipper about signing the divorce papers, though?"

"That's... Um, you see..." A good excuse evaded Hana's grasp. Her gaze darted about restlessly.

As she was dithering, Saku's hand shot out to grab her chin. He leaned in and kissed her. He wrapped his free hand around the back of her head, as if he knew what she was thinking, and blocked off her means of escape.

With no way to resist, Hana could only wait for Saku to have his fill.

He kissed her slow and deep, enjoying every moment. When he was satisfied, he leisurely pulled away from her, his lips quirked mischievously. His good mood made his grouchiness a second ago seem like a lie.

Hana was panting for breath and blushing fiercely. "Stupid Saku..." She had to muster all her energy to fling the insult.

"But you didn't hate it, right?" he said with an arrogant—and infuriating—grin.

However, he wasn't wrong. Hana was vexed that he'd seen through the fact that the kiss hadn't disgusted her.

As her one petty act of resistance, she wiped her mouth with the back of her hand.

"You wound me," he said.

"Just deserts!" she shouted. "You..." The kiss came flooding back to her mind. The dwindling heat in her body flared anew and rushed to her face.

"Did it feel good?" he teased.

"Idiot!"

Had there been any potential weapons in her immediate vicinity, she would've swung one down on Saku's head without question.

"Well, anyway, I'm serious." His tone went from playful to sober in an instant. "You should avoid going outside as much as possible."

Hana schooled her expression. "Is it that bad?"

"Several practitioners have already been killed."

She gulped.

"The culprits will stop at nothing," Saku continued. "People related to the five clans are in the most danger. I warned Mother and the others to be on their guard earlier as well."

"Doesn't that make you a target, too?" Hana asked.

"Who do you think I am?" he scoffed. "I'm the genius who obtained the Obsidian rank at the youngest age. I don't need you to worry about me."

Saku's nonchalant attitude did not assuage Hana's worries.

He smiled softly. "Be good." Then he kissed her again, a soft and fleeting touch of the lips, and got out of the car.

"You too, be careful, Saku."

Hana hadn't been able to come up with anything more helpful, but her uninspired words nevertheless brought a happy smile to Saku's face.

"I will," he said.

The door shut with a *thud*. The car pulled away, leaving Saku behind.

Hana watched Saku through the rear window, an anxious expression on her face, until he was completely out of sight.

◆

Several days after Hana had been ambushed by Kikiyo and Kiriya, Suzu rushed up to her excitedly the moment she arrived at school.

"Hey, Hana, did you hear? The third-year Class A is getting new transfer students today! They're from another branch of Obsidian High, I heard," Suzu said.

"Oh yeah?" Hana replied disinterestedly.

Suzu pouted. "Why aren't you more excited?"

"Why are you so excited in the first place?" retorted Hana. "Class A has nothing to do with us Class C-ers."

Class A regarded Class C as gum on the bottom of their shoe. It was an unspoken understanding among the Class C students that they shouldn't get involved with the other class, and that even if they were to, nothing good would happen. Unless it was urgent, they didn't go near the Class A classroom.

Class A students never bothered approaching Class C students, either, as the inferior class was beneath their notice.

"The transfer students are the grandchildren of the main Nijouin family, you know. And they're twins, like you and Hazuki," Suzu explained. "Did you know they've been nominated to become the next heads of the family? They must be amazing, don't you think?"

"Mmm."

The warmth of Suzu's enthusiastic chatter crashed up against Hana's frosty indifference.

It was only natural that Suzu was making a big deal of the transfer.

For a low-tier practitioner, the heads of the five clans were untouchable beings, people who were the natural targets of envy and admiration in equal measure.

When Hana took stock of their surroundings, she realized that the entire classroom was abuzz with talk about the transfer students.

Obsidian High, the school that all children from practitioner families had to attend, was actually a network of schools with branches in the regions each of the five clans was based in.

Hana went to Obsidian High School Campus One. The Nijouin twins were transferring from Obsidian High Campus Two.

"They might just be normal people, though," Hana said.

"Sure, maybe they're nothing the wife of the Ichinomiya lord would deign to fuss over," Suzu said.

"It's not like that. I haven't met any of the other heads besides Saku, either."

"Really?"

"Really. Oh, but I did meet the grandchildren of the Nijouin head recently. A girl and a guy, Kikiyo and Kiriya."

The moment the names were out of Hana's mouth, Suzu's expression turned surprised. She grabbed Hana's shoulder. "Those are the transfer students, Hana!"

"What? Seriously?"

The last time Hana had received such a large shock was when Suzu had announced she'd gotten a boyfriend.

There was the fact that the two were twins, but on top of that, she couldn't help but think that neither had seemed powerful enough to be candidates for the clan's succession. She especially couldn't imagine the mousy Kikiyo leading a clan.

With a person like her at the helm, the rest of the clan was sure to be ill at ease. Looking at it that way, it was possible that a willful and cocky person like Saku was actually well suited to be clan lord.

The clamor died down when their homeroom teacher walked in as the bell rang.

Homeroom flowed straight into first period.

Up until now, Hana had approached her classes with the same motivation as breaks, which was to say none at all. However, recently, she had started taking notes properly.

That wasn't anything to brag about—note-taking was normal for students—but it was a shocking sign of precipitous growth for Hana, whose definition of class equaled naptime.

Seeing Hana awake and scribbling seriously left a deep impression on her teachers, who remarked, "Are you finally going to take your classes seriously?" Her unusual behavior had sent shock waves through the teachers who taught Class C.

The extent to which Hana had avoided the path to becoming a practitioner until now became crystal clear.

Saku, who had been too busy as of late to spend any proper time with her, had threatened to report her to Mio instantly if she failed any of her upcoming exams, and Hana was desperate to avoid special tutoring sessions with her mother-in-law. During the break between classes, she copied borrowed notes from Suzu on the classes she'd skipped before.

"Hana, what's with the sudden zeal for studying?" Suzu asked.

"I'm gonna be a study demon until these tests are over and pass every single one," Hana swore.

"Eh? Isn't that asking for too much?"

The hurtful riposte from her best friend slashed Hana's rare burst of motivation.

"Suzuuu," she whined.

"Be real, Hana. You've failed every single exam since entering Obsidian High."

"Ugh, don't say that."

Back in her middle school days, out of a desire to be praised by her parents, Hana had gone so far as to sacrifice sleep for her studies and had gotten relatively good grades as a result.

However, after her parents gave up on her, studying became meaningless. She'd been putting in the bare minimum ever since.

Then she entered Obsidian High and was placed into Class C as she wanted to be, and the last grain of hope her parents had for her evaporated. Free from her parents' curse, she was able to do whatever she wanted. It was almost fascinating how sharply her grades plummeted. She hadn't bothered to hide it, either.

Her parents had been livid at first, but they soon turned their attention to Hazuki, which meant that, happily, Hana was free to ignore her classes and her studies as she liked. It was no surprise that Hana left a trail of failing grades in her wake.

It wasn't that she was stupid to begin with, but she was clearly lacking knowledge.

"I'm seriously in a pinch here! At this rate, I'm screwed," Hana complained. She was regretting marrying Saku more than ever. "Teach me, Suzu."

"No way. Impossible," Suzu said. "My grades aren't good, either. Besides, you have a sister in Class A."

"I'd ask her if I could," Hana muttered to herself, but her voice was too quiet to reach Suzu. Her friend tilted her head quizzically. "Never mind. Hazuki's in a different classroom, so it's not like I can go and ask her, right?"

"That's true. It's too high a hurdle for us to go over to Class A."

"Exactly."

Hana was relieved she'd hit on an explanation Suzu would accept. She hadn't told Suzu about the way she'd been treated in the Ichise house nor that she'd broken off relations with her family. That was why Suzu naturally assumed that since Hana and Hazuki were twins, they were close.

The ruse was helped along by the way Hazuki, in her role as a star student, tended to rebuke people who insulted Hana.

Hana had no intention of correcting Suzu's misunderstanding. She knew that if she did, she'd only end up worrying Suzu about her situation.

"What if you asked Lord Ichinomiya's younger brother?" Suzu smiled warmly, blissfully unaware of how insane her suggestion was.

Or was it?

"Brother? You mean Nozomu?" Hana asked.

"Wow, you don't address him by his title? Is that because he's your brother-in-law?"

"Oh, I guess."

Apparently, it was surprising for Suzu that Hana called the Ichinomiyas by their first names.

Of course, had Hana not known Saku, she wouldn't have been close enough to the main family to address them by name.

Saku had told her to call him by his name, but Nozomu hadn't said any such thing; she'd just ended up calling Nozomu whatever she wanted. In any case, it would've been strange for her to call Nozomu *young master* or what have you but address Saku, the lord of the clan, by his first name, husband or not.

Nozomu hadn't complained, so it was fine.

"There's an idea. Nozomu *is* in our grade," Hana mused.

If she skillfully used Saku as bait, Nozomu, with his hot-and-cold personality and secret brother complex, just might help her out.

"Is it time for the *magatama* to make its debut? Hmm."

She felt drained just thinking about being tutored by Nozomu, who only ever showed her his cold side. Plus, if they were to hold a study session in the Ichinomiya residence and Mio caught wind of it, she might find out about Hana's grades, too.

That would be awful.

Hana wanted to keep her grades a secret from Mio at all costs.

The day Mio found out would be the day her attendance in Mio's special tutoring sessions would become mandatory.

Hana buried her face in her arms. "This might be the end of the line for me…"

It was nearly time for the next period to begin, but just then, there was a ruckus in the hallway.

"What's going on?" Suzu asked.

"The boys are fooling around. What else?" Hana said. Her tone showed a clear lack of interest. The commotion had nothing to do with her.

In the next second, that ceased to be true.

"S-so this is where you were!"

The yell reverberated through the room, loud enough to startle even Hana, who looked up from the notes she was copying.

"Ah—" Hana gasped involuntarily after seeing the person who had barged into the room.

Standing at the door in the middle of the hubbub with an expression like she owned the place was the girl Hana had met the other day, Kikiyo.

Kiriya followed close behind her. Unlike his sister, who was, for some reason, on the verge of tears, he was wearing a poker face today, too.

What was even more surprising was that Hazuki, looking harried, came along with the twins into the classroom as well. The whispering among the Class C students grew more fevered.

"Huh? What are the Class A kids doing here?"

"Hazuki came, too. Lucky us!"

"Those are the transfer students everyone's talking about."

"Really? I wonder what they came for?"

Kikiyo ignored all the gossip and cut a path straight to Hana. "Why are you in Class C and not Class A?!" she demanded.

"What do you mean, 'why'? I've been in Class C since first year," Hana replied.

"You're Lord Ichinomiya's wife. Aren't you ashamed to be in Class C?!"

"Not at all."

It was a contractual marriage, after all. She hadn't a drop of motivation to learn for Saku's sake. She might have been making an effort toward her studies now, but that was for her, not for Saku.

"Well, you should be," Kikiyo said.

"Say what you want." But Hana was in a tough position, too.

On top of everything else, Kikiyo, as always, looked ready to cry. Even though she was doing the interrogating, from the outside, it seemed like *Hana* was bullying her.

"Did you do something to the new transfer student, Hana?" Suzu asked immediately, looking doubtfully at her friend.

"No, I'm perfectly innocent here, so don't misunderstand," Hana answered. "And you," she said to Kikiyo, "isn't it a little rude for you to barge in here all of a sudden? The class I'm in has nothing to do with you."

"Th-that might be true, but...but Lord Ichinomiya..." Kikiyo trailed off.

"Lord Ichionomiya warned you that this is a *private* issue for the Ichinomiya clan, didn't he?"

"Er..." Kikiyo was shaken by Hana's harsh reply, and tears started to pool in her eyes.

Suzu threw Hana a reproachful look. "Poor thing. You shouldn't bully her, Hana."

"I am obviously doing nothing of the sort!" Hana protested. "This is what she's always like."

Hana didn't know Kikiyo well enough to say anything about "*always*," but the girl had been dreadfully insecure the last time they'd met as well. Was that just her personality?

"Besides," Hana continued, "haven't you heard already that I haven't got a scrap of talent? Wasn't that why you came to confront me the other day, too? Because you don't approve of me?"

"You're not wrong," Kikiyo said, "but I didn't think you were so weak that you were in Class C. I went to Class A primed and ready, and you weren't there. Can you imagine the shock I received when I heard from Nozomu you were in Class C?"

"Not in the least," Hana said bluntly.

"Oh." Kikiyo deflated, her shoulders slumping.

Hana watched tears glaze Kikiyo's eyes. The question *Did you use teardrops?* was on the tip of her tongue, but she bit it back. It suddenly occurred to her that Kikyo reminded her of something, not that it mattered at the moment.

Kiriya, who'd been observing from the side, tapped his sister's shoulder. "Let's go," he said, spare with his words, and gestured to the door.

The teacher was standing there with a vexed expression, unable to enter the classroom even though it was time to start class. If he had been watching the whole time, he ought to have told the twins off. Surely, Hana wasn't the only one thinking that.

Why are you being such a pushover?

She wanted him to do his job and reprimand the twins properly, but she guessed that their teacher had calculated it was too much of a risk to scold the two people who were candidates to become the next heads of the Nijouin clan and incur their ire. Obsidian High was a private school operated by the five clans. For a teacher employed by the school, confronting the twins of the Nijouin main family may have been too daunting an ask.

Hazuki had likely come along to stop the twins as well, but she was at a loss for what to do as well. What in the world had she come for?

Hana looked at her sister, whom she hadn't crossed paths with in a while. Hazuki was looking back at her.

When their gazes met, Hazuki was the first to avert her eyes, turning away immediately. Hana felt like Hazuki was shunning her very existence, and a nameless emotion surged up within her.

She wanted to ask for details about the incident the other day when Hazuki had lost control of her powers, but Hazuki didn't seem like she'd be open to speaking.

They were twins, but unlike Kikiyo and Kiriya, who had a tight-knit relationship, Hana and Hazuki couldn't be further apart.

But Hana's own actions were to blame for that.

She had chosen her own peace and comfort over Hazuki.

What could she possibly say to Hazuki after making the decision she did?

"Kikiyo, Kiriya, let's go back to class," Hazuki said.

Kikiyo looked apologetic. "Yes. I apologize for the trouble. I acted without thinking..." Maybe she was aware of the bother she'd been to the people around her. She trailed off and left alongside Kiriya, who remained expressionless.

They could finally begin class, but Hana doubted this would be the end. She sighed softly.

Chapter 3

Kikiyo and Kiriya's transfer brought subtle changes to Hana's school life.

"Hana, they're here again," one of her classmates reported.

"Ugh," Hana groaned.

With a faintly beleaguered expression, she looked toward the classroom entrance, where someone was staring fixedly at her without saying a word.

That someone was Kikiyo.

Since the other girl had found out that Hana was in Class C, she had been stopping by during breaks between classes, not to speak to Hana but just to spy.

At first, she had attracted attention since she was both a Class A student and a direct descendant of the Nijouin bloodline, but after several days, the other Class C students had gotten used to her presence. Now whenever she stopped by, the only reaction the students had was "Again?"

Next to Kikiyo, Kiriya was fiddling with his phone—the picture of disinterest.

If he was going to tag along with Kikiyo, Hana wished he would do her the favor of taking his sister back to their classroom. Hana wondered what he was thinking as he played accomplice to his sister's bizarre actions.

It would've been more productive for the twins to make friends with the Class A students than to keep an eye on Hana.

Nonetheless, Kikiyo insisted on sticking to Hana.

Did she like Saku that much?

But Saku didn't show a shred of the same interest. It was sad to think all this was one-sided on Kikiyo's part.

Kikiyo, with her large, tearful eyes that were tinged with resentment, reminded Hana of something.

Ah, that was it.

She looked like Suzu's squirrel shikigami.

Suzu's shikigami never wanted to fight. Whenever Suzu had to call upon her shikigami's powers, the shikigami would turn an entreating gaze on Suzu. Then when Suzu refused to listen, the shikigami's cute, round eyes would fill with bitterness. Kikiyo's expression was an uncanny match.

Having figured out the mystery, Hana felt satisfied, like she'd finally managed to cough up a small bone that had gotten lodged in her throat.

The twins hovered in the doorway until the bell rang to signal the start of the next period. At last, Kiriya moved.

"Kikiyo, let's go," he said.

"Yes…" She nodded obediently. Reluctant to leave, she gave Hana one last glance before returning to her own class.

"Seriously, what do they keep coming for?" Hana muttered.

If they had something to say, they should just say it.

Or was it that they *couldn't* say it?

Saku had warned them that he would report them to the lord of the Nijouin clan if they messed with Hana further, so they had to be careful with their words.

How frightening was the clan lord—the twins' grandfather?

Hana had never met him, so she could only try to imagine what the man was like. What came to mind was a severe person like Mio.

According to Suzu, he was an elderly man in his seventies.

Hana was Saku's wife, yet she knew less than Suzu about the five clans. That could be a problem.

At this rate, she was going to end up enrolled in Mio's special tutoring sessions for sure. The thought made her blood run cold.

"Ugh, I don't have time to be distracted, but it's impossible to concentrate with *those two* stalking me every hour," complained Hana.

"It's impossible for you to score above the average either way. Give up and hang out with me instead," Suzu said blithely.

How can you curse me with such misfortune while wearing such a soft smile?

"Suzuuu. Stop tempting me. I'm seriously doomed if I don't pass."

"Nope, no way. Not for you, Hana. There's a ninety-nine point nine percent chance that you'll fail."

"It hurts that I can't deny it…" Hana clenched both fists in her hair in frustration. Even if her chances were slim, she couldn't afford to stop studying. "It'll be all right. I'm the type that can do it if I try!" Hana said. "…Theoretically." The last word tacked onto her proclamation betrayed her insecurity.

Hana was backed up against the wall, but during lunch break, as if to foil her study efforts further, an incident occurred.

At lunch, Hana was slurping down udon while reading her textbook, a perfect example of bad manners.

Suzu was sitting across from her. Seeing drops of soup from Hana's noodles fly onto the textbook bothered her and soured her mood. "Come on, Hana," she said, "take a break from studying at least while we're eating."

Hana shot her down. "I don't have any time to waste. The exams are right around the corner."

"That's true, but still." Suzu was displeased that Hana wouldn't even chat with her.

"I'll make it up to you. After the exams, let's go somewhere," Hana offered.

"Yay! Really? I'm excited. It's been so long since we've gone anywhere together. You've been poor company lately."

"Sorry. Saku told me to restrain myself."

"Well, I suppose it can't be helped if the head of the clan ordered it."

Suzu was from a practitioner family, so the idea that the clan lord's word was absolute had been hammered into her from an early age. Once Hana brought Saku into the picture, Suzu accepted the situation readily.

"I hope everything gets resolved soon...," Hana said.

She had yet to hear any good news from Saku about the spelled-talismans' recovery.

He was still buried up to his neck in work, so it seemed that the case would take a while longer to resolve.

Geez. Can people stop causing so much trouble? Prevented from taking her detours on the way home, Hana's stress had been steadily building, along with her resentment toward those Skull of Nirvana goons.

Finished with her udon, Hana placed her palms together to show thanks for the meal. "That hit the spot," she said. She tidied up her bowl and cutlery and stood up.

"Oh, Hana, wait for me," Suzu said.

"Take your time. I'm heading back to the classroom to study."

Her friend made a sullen expression. "Awww. I wanted to keep talking."

She felt apologetic, but she only smiled wryly and said, "How about you study with me?"

"Whaaat?" Suzu's face twisted in distaste.

"Hear me out," Hana interjected. "You want to join the Association of Practitioners after graduating, right? Well, the Association takes grades into account, doesn't it?"

Half the students in the school had their sights on the Association, so their teachers had been harping on about the academic requirements since they were first-years.

"That's that, and this is this," Suzu said, her gaze slipping away from Hana.

Apparently, it didn't matter that good grades were important. She hated the idea of studying.

"Besides, I plan to join the rear support. Everything will work out even if I'm not good at studying," she said, self-assured. Where in the world did her confidence come from?

Then…

"The world of practitioners isn't so forgiving."

…words of rebuke flew from the voyeur who had been keeping her distance thus far: Kikiyo. Hana hadn't noticed her arrival.

Next to her was, no need to guess, Kiriya. His black pupils, which revealed nothing of what he was thinking, were trained on Ha— Suzu.

"Everyone in the Association, including the practitioners in rear support, fight to protect this country at the risk of their lives. Your frivolous attitude mocks that resolution, and I cannot abide it." The shrinking violet had up and disappeared. Kikiyo's expression showed her anger.

Suzu's nonchalant statement had made light of practitioners and seemed to have touched a sore spot.

Kikiyo's lecture wasn't over. "You, too, were born into a practitioner's family, were you not? How can you scoff at the rear support so easily? As part of the five clans, which are responsible for all practitioners, I'll not forgive it."

Scolded by Kikiyo, Suzu curled in on herself and apologized. "I hadn't meant to... I was careless. I'm sorry, truly."

Suzu's despondency and apology assuaged Kikiyo. "Very well, as long as you are aware. I apologize for speaking so harshly all of a sudden." She bowed deeply to Suzu.

Flustered, Suzu jerked to her feet and bowed back. "Er, ah, me too. Sorry!"

Hana watched the two of them—mirrored in their posture—with indifference. Whatever they were doing, it had nothing to do with her. But that changed the moment Kikyo straightened and turned her gaze toward Hana.

"Hana. You, I cannot accept. Someone in Class C is not fit to be Lord Ichinomiya's wife," Kikiyo proclaimed.

"Well, good thing I'm not looking for your approval," Hana replied.

Saku had required Hana's power to restore the barrier around the pillar. That was all Hana needed to know.

Regardless of what Kikiyo said, Hana had already been recognized within the Ichinomiya household.

Admittedly, Nozomu was an exception, but he wasn't a serious problem. He may act tough, but he was squishy on the inside.

Kikiyo continued, "I want to know why Lord Ichinomiya chose someone like you."

"What do you intend to do?" Hana regarded Kikiyo warily.

The other girl was different than usual. Her typical shyness was nowhere to be seen. Instead, she projected a courage that hinted at inner strength.

Kikiyo pointed her finger at Hana and declared in the middle of the crowded cafeteria, "I challenge you to a shikigami duel!"

The surrounding conversations had cut off as the students around them had turned to watch the situation unfold, so Kikiyo's voice carried clearly through the quiet room.

An uproar erupted in the cafeteria, the students clamoring over one another.

"Wait, she said 'duel,' but anyone can see who the victor will be."

"Seriously, though. We're talking about the scraps of the Ichise family here."

"Isn't her shikigami some sort of bug?"

"A duel with Hazuki would be one thing, but Hana has no chance. I almost feel sorry for her."

It was open season on Hana.

No one believed the good-for-nothing Hana could win.

Of course, Hana had kept her powers hidden precisely to keep herself off everyone's radar, so their incredulity was inevitable.

Saku had seen through her in an instant, though. He wasn't an Obsidian rank for nothing.

To put it another way, there wasn't a single person in the school—teachers included—who was strong enough to figure out Hana's true ability.

Kikiyo and Kiriya, the candidates to be the next heads of the Nijouin clan, were no exception, either.

In response to Kikiyo, Hana said, "Don't want to."

"You have no right to refuse. You will fight," Kikiyo snapped. "With Kiriya."

"..." *You're challenging me to a duel with someone else?!* Hana couldn't be the only one questioning the situation.

"You're the one who threw down the gauntlet, but you're leaving your twin to clean up the mess?" Hana asked incredulously.

"I can't stand insects. I get goose bumps just thinking about them."

Kikiyo rubbed her arms, her face set in grim lines. It seemed like she was serious.

But Hana adored Azuha. Her lips flattened into a line. "Azuha might be a butterfly, but she's gorgeous!" Azuha flew to land on Hana's finger. "Take a proper look at these beautiful rainbow wings. See how they shimmer." Hana shoved her hand toward Kikiyo.

The girl let out an agonized shriek. "Eek! Get away, get away!"

"How rude." Hana sniffed, as indignant as a mother whose child had been scorned.

Kiriya moved to stand in front of Hana and said, "If you please." He bowed deeply, straightened, and proffered his hand.

Hana reflexively reached out to grab it. "Okay, sure?"

At that moment, Kikiyo's eyes lit up. "Just now, you shook Kiriya's hand! That means you accept our challenge!"

"Wha—? No, that's not what I meant at all," protested Hana.

"No. I won't let you run away anymore," Kikiyo said.

Kiriya was awfully polite for someone whose facial muscles hardly ever twitched, and Hana had responded to his courtesy without thinking. Thanks to Hana's slip, Kikiyo was brimming with enthusiasm.

Kikiyo was richly emotive, and her expressions changed on a dime. It was a mystery why her twin, Kiriya, had no expressions at all.

Their personalities were so different, it was questionable whether they were twins at all.

Not that Hana could really talk.

Hana and Hazuki. While they shared the same appearance, they were polar opposites, a fact that both they and everyone around them knew.

"Let's go to the courtyard," Kikiyo said.

"I'm not doing it. I'm serious," Hana refuted.

"No, you will fight. If you refuse, I'll ask the principal. I know he'll fold under a bit of pressure."

"You play dirty for someone with such a cute face."

"You're giving me no other choice!!" Kikiyo objected, half in tears.

Hana was at the end of her rope. She looked around at the others for help, but there were no courageous souls willing to face the Nijouin clan and come to Hana's rescue.

She didn't know what to do.

But then she spotted Nozomu out of the corner of her eye and drawled, "Golly gee, is that Nozomu I spy?"

Nozomu's face scrunched like he'd been spotted by someone repugnant. Hana paid no mind to his annoyed stare, ran up to him, and laid a hand on his shoulder.

"Deary me. I, your feeble sister-in-law, am in a pinch. Of course you'll help me out, right?"

"Whatever. Do what you want. It's got nothing to do with me," he scoffed, coldly shrugging off her hand. He turned to leave the cafeteria.

Hana didn't panic. In fact, quite the opposite. A malicious smile rose to her face, and she took out the white-agate *magatama* charm from her pocket.

"Awww, boo, that's too bad. If you helped me out, I was going to give you this *magatama*. It's a matching pair with Saku's, you know…*and* the white agate strengthens the bond between siblings, but alas," Hana said, her words full of faux sincerity.

Nozomu was already a distance away, but he spun on his heel and came charging back.

Hana smirked.

"You're not lying, are you?" he demanded.

Hana knew exactly what he meant, but she played dumb anyway. "Hmmm. About what?"

Nozomu shoved himself forward, a ghastly expression on his face.

"About it matching my brother's!" His voice trembled, but it was as soft as a whisper. He probably didn't want word about his brother complex to get out. That was part of what made this so enjoyable.

"Scout's honor," Hana said. "He wears it together with his Association pendant. You haven't seen it?"

His face brightened with recognition. "Oh, that!"

"Yes, *that*. This *magatama* is a pair with his. The white agate helps foster a deeper connection between siblings. The effect is sure to double if you each have one," Hana whispered to Nozomu for emphasis.

"A deeper connection..."

Nozomu's case of brother complex must've been particularly severe. His eyes were locked onto the white stone Hana was holding. When she moved it left to right, his gaze followed.

She brought the hand holding the *magatama* to a perfect stop and dangled the pendant at Nozomu's eye level. "Want it?"

"What do you want for it?" he demanded.

Apparently, Nozomu wasn't even going to try to hide his brother complex from her. It took all of Hana's strength not to laugh.

"You'll help out your beloved sister-in-law and fight in my stead, right?"

Nozomu's eyes flicked toward Kiriya before returning to rest on Hana. The corner of his lips lifted. "Sure."

He stood in front of Kiriya and lifted a finger to point at the other boy. "I'll be your opponent!" he declared, his voice ringing.

Hana applauded. "There's the kind younger brother who always thinks of his sister! I expected nothing less."

The turn of events greatly flustered Kikiyo, who had initiated the whole thing. "Hold on. Wait a minute! That's not what we discussed."

"What are you talking about?" Nozomu said flatly. "You have your champion. You can hardly complain about us doing the same."

"Guh—but I..." Kikiyo could not refute Nozomu's argument.

"You picked a fight with the lady of the Ichinomiya clan. Well, I'm the clan lord's younger brother, and I'll be footing the bill today."

"Uh, um, what do we do, Kiriyaaa?" Her plan having gone off the rails, Kikiyo grabbed Kiriya's arm, looking as if she was about to cry.

Kiriya placed a hand on Kikiyo's head to calm her down. "You were the one to propose the duel, so there's nothing we can do now."

"Nooo, et tu, Kiriya," Kikiyo moaned.

Kiriya glanced around the cafeteria and added, "It may be too late to put a stop to this."

The other students were frenzied with excitement.

"Oh, wow, a duel between an Ichinomiya and a Nijouin!"

"Are they gonna do it now? What about next period?"

"Ditch, duh! If you let this chance go, you may never get another one in your entire life."

"Oh my god, I'm pumped!"

"You're not the one fighting, idiot. All right, okay, but I know what you mean. Come on, we gotta hurry up and finish eating."

"Yeah! Or all the good spots will be taken."

The clamor that filled the cafeteria made the silence from a few minutes ago seem like a dream.

Some of the students started to wolf down their food, some took out their phones to message people who weren't there about the developments, and some bolted for the courtyard to secure a front-row seat.

The situation was blowing up to be way bigger than Hana had expected.

With the atmosphere as charged as it was, it didn't seem like Kikiyo nor anyone else would be able to put on the brakes.

"It seems like there's no choice but to go ahead with it," Hana said.

"Ugh, there's no point if you're not the one fighting," Kikiyo whined.

However, unlike Kikiyo, Hana was relieved that the spotlight had shifted from her onto Nozomu and Kiriya's duel instead.

"Hey," Nozomu said to Hana, "I'll fight on your behalf, but you better not forget my compensation."

"I got it, I got it. As long as you win… Heh-heh-heh." Hana chuckled meaningfully with a smirk like a corrupt politician.

Satisfied—or perhaps creeped out by Hana's expression—Nozomu turned back to face Kiriya. "The faster this headache is dealt with, the better," he said. "Let's take this outside."

Kiriya nodded and followed Nozomu. Behind him trailed Kikiyo, her shoulders slumped.

Hana tagged along at the end, cheerful now that Kikiyo's attack had been deflected toward someone else.

The duel was to take place in the schoolyard.

Because shikigami duels were held during practicals, there was already a court there.

Students lined up around the white lines demarcating the bounds. There were too many people for everyone to see, so there were spectators crowding around the second-floor windows of the school building as well.

No one complained about missing their next class.

Besides, scattered among the audience waiting in heart-pounding excitement were teachers as well. Even the principal had shown up.

Likely, the entire student body had come out to watch the duel.

What started as a private confrontation had blown into a school-wide affair. The train had gone off the rails. Surely, there was no stopping it now.

Photographers and reporters from the newspaper club had taken the spots with the very best views. News of the fight was going to be splashed all over the next day's edition.

"How did this happen…?" Kikiyo groaned to herself, her hands in her hair. Apparently, she hadn't foreseen the duel growing into such a big deal.

With this level of commotion, there would be no preventing the news from reaching Saku's ears. Considering Saku had already told her off once, the prospect must have had her stomach in knots.

Kikiyo was only reaping what she sowed, but Hana figured the least she could do was give the girl some stomach medicine.

"Who do you think will win, Master?" Azuha asked, her voice melting into the din of the crowd. Only Hana heard her.

"Hmmm, if Saku was the one fighting, I'd have no doubt Saku would win, but this is Nozomu we're talking about," Hana said.

When Hana had fought him, Azuha had won easily without taking a single hit. Hana's regard for Nozomu's abilities was not high.

On top of that, the top student of Class A was Hazuki. Nozomu was merely a runner-up at best.

In comparison, Kiriya had been nominated as a candidate to be the next clan lord, according to Suzu's sources.

Hana wasn't sure how talented Kiriya actually was, but judging by the implications, he must be at least on par with Nozomu.

Was it possible that despite his candidacy, he wasn't really that strong? Or perhaps, was he hiding his true abilities the way Hana was?

"Kiriya is a mystery. It could go either way," she finally concluded.

The two young men faced each other on the court. Nozomu was fired up, driven by the thought of winning the *magatama* pendant that matched his brother's. By contrast, Kiriya was staring vacantly at the clouds drifting overhead. It was unclear whether he had any motivation at all.

"Yeeeah, I seriously have no clue what kind of person he is. He's like a puzzle," Hana said.

Kiriya was the opposite of Kikiyo, whose thoughts were written on her face, plain and easy for all to read. His personality was hard to grasp, and so was his fighting style.

Nozomu would be doing the actual fighting, so for all intents and purposes, there was no reason for Hana to worry about it, but she couldn't help but wonder.

After a while, the two combatants finished their preparations. The judge was the physical-education teacher—a man whose most attractive feature was his muscles, which bulged underneath his clothing, and who was more excited than anyone else about the match.

With his massive bulk, he was a Red-rank practitioner, third of the five ranks. He had a wealth of experience and had been dispatched from the Association of Practitioners to teach in the school. Not that any of that information was relevant at the moment.

He was a true muscle head, so he should judge the match fairly.

"Are you ready? Fighters, summon your shikigami," he declared.

"Guren, show yourself," Nozomu commanded. His hawk shikigami materialized, circling overhead.

"Hibari." Kiriya mumbled what sounded like a name. A magnificent panther appeared and nuzzled Kiriya's hand sweetly.

Kiriya stroked the panther, his lips relaxing marginally from their usual flat line.

"Wow, so his shikigami is a panther?" Hana mused.

The energy pouring off it was palpable.

But Hana knew the strongest of all practitioners, and she couldn't help comparing Kiriya with Saku. As she had thought, the boy didn't seem powerful enough to be a candidate for clan lord. She tilted her head quizzically.

The same could be said about his other half, Kikiyo. They were certainly strong compared with the other Class A students. That was no surprise for direct descendants of one of the five clans. But were they capable of defending the pillar, a task that even Saku had struggled with?

Granted, whoever succeeded the Nijouin clan wasn't Hana's concern.

"Fight!"

While Hana was zoning out, preoccupied with other thoughts, the PE teacher gave the green light. She snapped back to the situation at hand.

Nozomu went on offense right away. "Guren!" he shouted.

Guren stopped circling and dropped into a precipitous dive, heading straight for Kiriya's panther. The panther jumped, anticipating the attack, and twisted its pliable body around to scratch Guren with its sharp claws. The hawk spat out a ball of energy that fended off the panther's claws.

Having deflected the attack, Guren escaped back into the sky, its home domain.

Then it rained a flurry of energy bursts down on the earth. The panther dodged with quick steps. When Guren swooped down low, the panther pounced on the opportunity and snapped at the hawk with its jaws. Guren spun to avoid the attack and managed to sink its talons into the panther's flank.

"Gwar!" The panther howled in pain, stumbling and falling to the ground.

However, it wasted no time regaining its footing. Guren had intended to launch a follow-up attack, but seeing its opponent recover, it immediately changed directions and flew up into the air instead.

The audience was following the exchange avidly and was rowdy with excitement.

"GO!"

"Damn, that was awesome."

"Just what you'd expect from direct descendants of the five clans. They're built different."

"I know, seriously. What's with the way their shikigami move? They're so COOL."

The students watched the two duelists with admiration.

The teachers were impressed by the display, too. A few even clapped.

In the midst of all the excitement, the photographers for the newspaper club were spamming the shutter button, hoping to get the perfect shot.

"Make sure to get some good ones!"

"Leave it to us!"

The camera geeks might have been the most riled up of all.

Hana decided to get some distance and tuck herself into a corner. When she walked away from the match, she was approached by Kikiyo, who had given up the front row as well.

"Shouldn't you watch your other half fight?" Hana asked.

Kikiyo looked sullen for whatever reason. "That was cowardly," she said in a low voice.

"What was?"

"Pulling in a bystander and running away! I wanted to see how powerful you were." She pursed her lips in frustration, perhaps dissatisfied that the duel hadn't gone according to plan.

Hana looked at Kikiyo with exasperation. "You're the one who sprang all this on me. I was just minding my own business. You have no right to talk," she retorted.

Tears welled up in Kikiyo's eyes. "But normally, people conduct themselves properly in order to gain recognition, don't they? I don't see you doing anything to help Lord Ichinomiya. That's why I thought you'd be motivated if I challenged you to fight. How did things get so out of hand? Why is Nozomu the one fighting?!"

Hana understood what Kikiyo wanted to say, but the last part of her tirade was just venting.

"Why do I need your approval anyway?" Hana said.

"Er, because otherwise…"

"Otherwise, *you* would be inconvenienced, right? You won't be able to give up on Saku as long as I'm so useless. But that has nothing to do with me. That's your problem; am I wrong?"

Kikiyo couldn't come up with a response. Her gaze flitted about restlessly, as if she were a lost child.

"If you like him, why don't you just confess? I think you'd be better off hearing how he feels in his own words, no?"

A direct approach would be infinitely better than Kikiyo's roundabout scrimmages with Hana.

But more to the point, Hana didn't want to get any more wrapped up with the twins than she already had been.

Declarations of battle day after day would drive her up the wall.

"C-c-c-con— Do you—? I don't!" Kikiyo stuttered.

Hana bit back the urge to snap, *What are you, a rooster?*

Kikiyo's face had turned so red, it looked painful. Deeply shaken, she hid her face in her hands.

"If you have the guts to offer me a three-billion-yen bribe, it'd be more productive to put that energy into talking with Saku, don't you think?"

Kikiyo shook her head so hard that it seemed like her head would fly off her neck. "No way! That's impossible!"

"But would you really be satisfied if I broke up with Saku? Could you really accept Hazuki becoming his next wife? I, for one, don't think so. You'd just carry on nitpicking at her flaws, no? *If I was Saku's wife, I'd would do such-and-such better.*"

"I…"

"Well, you probably don't want to hear any of this from me, seeing as I'm currently married to him and all." Hana shrugged. "But you're not gonna feel any better by attacking me, right?" Behind her words was a rebuke: *Don't you think you're directing your energy at the wrong person?*

"..." Kikiyo looked down at the ground, silent.

A moment later, the crowd around them burst into wild applause.

"Amaaazing! It's Ichinomiya's win!"

"Nozomu's awesome!"

"Hold on a minute. But the Nijouin twin was cool as hell, too."

It appeared that the battle had been settled while Hana and Kikiyo were talking.

And Nozomu had won. What a shocking turn of events.

Hana would have to throw a few words of praise his way. He would probably swat her away for the bother, though.

Hana left Kikiyo—who remained frozen—behind and went over to Nozomu.

The fighting had turned fierce when she hadn't been paying attention. The surface of the court was left gouged and cracked.

"Hmmm, maybe I should've stayed and watched."

Opportunities to watch a battle between two descendants of the five clans were few and far between—all the more so since Hana was in a different class.

The audience began to scatter now that the duel was over. Nozomu was crouching on the ground in the middle of the crowd.

Having expended his energy in the fight, he was somewhat listless.

"Are you okay?" Hana asked.

"Where'd you run off to after dumping your fight on me?" Nozomu's usual fire was nowhere to be seen. How remarkable.

"My bad, my bad. The cameramen were all gung ho about filming the match. I didn't want to get in their way."

"Stuff like that isn't worth the trouble. Those hyenas always find a way to sneak in." He had no kind words about the newspaper club. Perhaps he had tussled with them in the past.

"More importantly, good job winning that duel," Hana said, "with the candidate for the next Nijouin clan lord as your opponent, no less," Hana said.

"It's *because* he's a Nijouin that I managed to eke out a win," Nozomu said.

"What?" Hana tilted her quizzically. She didn't know a thing about the five clans.

Nozomu's expression turned exasperated. "You're the lady of the Ichinomiya clan! You shouldn't need additional explanation."

"You can't expect me to learn everything overnight. I'm in the middle of studying. So out with it. Why?"

Nozomu still looked fed up, but he sighed and explained briefly, "The Nijouin clan specializes in crafting talismans. Of course, they're expected to demonstrate a certain level of raw power, but brute strength is not the primary requirement to become the Nijouin clan lord."

"So you mean those twins are candidates because they're talented at making talismans?"

"Probably. They haven't noticed the powers you're hiding even though Saku noticed right away. The candidates for the other clans' heads will likely all react differently to you as well." Nozomu seemed somewhat bitter. He hadn't been able to gauge Hana's true ability when they had met, either.

As Hana was pondering whether Nozomu was still hung up over his loss to her, Nozomu stuck out his hand. Hana instinctively took it. Did he want a victory handshake?

"Ngh," Hana groaned as Nozomu flung her hand away.

"Wrong!" he yelled and held out his hand again. "Gimme that. You know. *That.*"

"That?" What in the world was he going on about? Question marks sprouted in Hana's mind.

A vein pulsed in Nozomu's forehead. "The *magatama*!" he demanded roughly.

"Ohhh! Right, right." Hana had completely forgotten. She placed the reward for his victory in his palm.

Nozomu cupped the *magatama* with both hands, holding it tenderly. His expression was jubilant.

"If you like your brother that much, why do you speak to him so spitefully?" Hana asked.

"Y-you've got it wrong!" he protested.

"What's the point in trying to hide it now? Keep making that guilty face, and everyone's gonna find out your secret. You know, Saku would probably be pleased if you were genuine with him."

"My feelings would only weigh him down."

"Where's your proof?"

"I mean, come on, I'm just a burden to him…" The words tumbled out of Nozomu's mouth, laden with self-deprecation. "There's no way Saku isn't ashamed to have a lousy brother like me. I was born into the main Ichinomiya family, but I'm no good. Defective. Not even worthy of being his rival."

Nozomu's expression darkened, but he kept his face downturned. In her mind, the downtrodden Nozomu overlapped with her past self, and her awful memories came rushing back.

An embarrassment to the family.

The older siblings' scraps.

Their family's shameful burden.

She had been called every one of those things by others before.

Hana took a deep breath to steady herself and shake off the tendrils of dark emotions pulling at her from the past. Then she karate-chopped Nozomu's head.

She landed a beautiful critical hit. In agony, Nozomu brought both hands to press against his forehead.

"Ow— You, what are you doing?!" he yelled, enraged by the unexpected attack.

She grabbed him by the lapels. This time, she head-butted him.

However, she took damage as well. Suffering from the pain of the blow, she brought up her hands to mirror Nozomu's in camaraderie.

"Ouch," she groaned.

"What's your problem?!"

"You were spouting nonsense, you brat, so I taught you a lesson."

"Who are you calling a brat?!"

"It's because you act like this that I'm calling you a brat!" She glared at him with tears in her eyes. "I don't know what delusions you're laboring under, but Saku isn't such a petty, narrow-minded man."

Nozomu was quiet. Her furious censure blew away his response.

"Did Saku tell you that? That you're a burden? That you're lousy?" she demanded.

"He wouldn't say anything like that!"

"Yeah, exactly! So you *do* know."

Nozomu's face twisted in confusion. He still didn't understand what Hana was trying to say.

"Saku may be arrogant, full of himself, and act like he's the center of the universe, but he's not the kind of guy who would say things to hurt other people," Hana said. "You're not as strong as Saku? You're not fit to be his rival? Of course you're not. Saku's cocky because he's put in the effort to deserve it. But his sense of responsibility is just as strong. He has the future of the country in his hands."

A practitioner charged with the protection of the pillar. That was the lord of the Ichinomiya clan.

He supported the country behind the scenes, where no one could see.

How heavy was the burden bearing down upon his shoulders?

Hana couldn't even imagine.

"What Saku cares about is his responsibilities and duties as the clan lord. Who's stronger, who would win—he doesn't make those comparisons. His mind is full of how to protect what's his. The difference between you and him starts with your resolve as practitioners."

Nozomu bit his lip in frustration.

"If Saku was in your position, he would invest the time you spend wavering into polishing his skills. He's part of the Ichinomiya clan, which is responsible for the pillar's protection, after all. And one of the people under his wing is you, his younger brother."

"...Shit—"

"There's no way Saku is embarrassed by you. There are few people who are as warm and passionate as him."

He might not have looked like it at first glance.

But there was no way a person who could risk their life for strangers could be unfeeling.

Nozomu gripped fistfuls of his hair, hiding his face behind his hands and arms.

For a while, all was silent.

Then Nozomu looked up. "Resolve... I see. Compared with my brother, my resolve as a practitioner is lacking?" He let out a self-deprecating laugh before climbing slowly to his feet and disappearing into the school building.

Hana watched him go without speaking. She sighed as she stood and dusted off her uniform. "Good grief, raising a kid is tough work."

Azuha came fluttering out and landed on Hana's finger. "What a minefield."

"Tell me about it."

"But you're in no position to talk."

"Azuha, you don't need to rub salt in the wound," Hana said. "I had the same thought when I reflected on what I'd said. *Look who's talking.*"

Waste of space. The elder sister's scraps. Bottom of the barrel.

The one most sensitive to those insults was Hana herself.

She felt embarrassed that she had mouthed off about practitioners' resolve when she hadn't a drop of it herself.

"Good thing no one's around to hear," she remarked.

Not a single person was left around her. From the bottom of her heart, she was relieved that the only ones who'd witnessed the latest page of her history in Obsidian High were Nozomu and Azuha.

That evening, Saku came back unusually early.

When he returned, Hana asked, "Could it be that you caught the terrorists?"

"No, not yet," he answered.

"Oh, I see."

"You sound disappointed," Saku said. "Were you lonely while I was gone?"

"Not at all."

Actually, the reason for Hana's crestfallen expression was that she couldn't go out and have fun while the Skull of Nirvana was still on the loose and the talismans were missing.

However, her rapid-fire rejection had been a misstep.

In the next moment, Saku's lips jerked into a stiff smile. "You're not going to reward your husband, who's been laboring outside all day?"

He prowled forward, closing the distance between him and Hana and crowding her up against the wall.

"Hang on, calm down," Hana said.

"I am calm."

Trapped between the wall and Saku, Hana no longer had any means of escape. She was dismayed.

"Don't you think it's the responsibility of a new wife to welcome her husband home from work with at least one measly, little kiss?" Saku said.

"I haven't heard of anything like that!" protested Hana.

"In that case, I declare it an Ichinomiya house rule from today on."

"No one needs such a rule!"

"Enough talking. Snap to it. A kiss for your beloved husband upon his return home," Saku ordered.

Pinned against the wall, Hana scrambled for an escape route. That was when Nozomu came stomping toward them, hollering, "Saku!"

Nozomu stopped next to his brother with a glower on his face. "I...I...," he stuttered.

Saku asked, "What's wrong?"

"I love you, Saku!" he declared.

The sudden confession had both Hana's and Saku's eyes wide as saucers.

Nozomu wasn't done. "That's why I'm going to be a top-notch practitioner and become your right-hand man! I'm an Ichinomiya, just like you!"

Having said his piece, he turned around and fled, his cheeks flushed with embarrassment.

"What the hell is up with him?" Saku said.

"Ah, I think he's leveled up from having a secret brother complex to just a regular brother complex," Hana replied.

"I didn't understand a word you said."

"It must be a shock."

Hana didn't know what kind of emotional changes Nozomu had undergone, but having given up on hiding his love for his brother, he had looked at peace. She figured he would be fine.

As for Hana, she astutely leaped at the opportunity afforded to her by the derailment and slipped out of the cage of Saku's arms.

Saku looked peeved, but he changed the topic. "Never mind that. What's this I hear about you fighting with the Nijouin twins?"

"Oh, so you heard the news, too?"

"Yeah. I know the broad strokes, though I don't know how Nozomu ended up in the fight," he said. "All this after I warned Kikiyo off, too. She had the audacity to ignore me? Well, I'll do what needs to be done. I'll have words with the Nijouin clan lord."

Contrary to his firm declaration, his expression was stormy. He seemed reluctant to follow through.

"You don't have to go that far," Hana said. "I KO'd her today."

Considering the verbal beating Hana had given Kikiyo, the other girl wasn't likely to get involved with Hana any more than necessary going forward.

"Hold up, don't do anything *I'm* going to have to apologize for, all right? I'm begging you."

"I haven't touched a hair on her head yet." Hana gave him a big thumbs-up. "Relax."

Saku's eyebrow twitched. "Yet? What do you mean, '*yet*'?!" he roared. "How am I supposed to relax after hearing that?!"

"You got yourself into this mess. There's no way you don't know, right?" Hana chided. "About how that girl feels about you."

"Sure, I *know*, but if she doesn't make a move, there's nothing I can do, either. And these other ways she's finding to air her pent-up emotions put me in a tough spot, too."

"What a heartbreaker you are."

"I am indeed a man among men. I permit you to fall head over heels for me," he said with a confident smirk.

Hana stamped on his foot and ground down viciously before turning a cold stare on him and saying, "Hurry up and do your job already."

◆

The next day, copies of the school newspaper were posted on the blackboards of every single classroom.

The text blared, DISTINGUISHED SONS OF THE ICHINOMIYAS AND NIJOUINS DUKE IT OUT! and THE GODDESS OF VICTORY BESTOWED HER FAVOR ON ICHINOMIYA!

A copy was posted in Hana's class, too. Her classmates swarmed around it the moment they arrived at school.

Hana had only come in a minute ago herself. Suzu walked up to her, smiling warmly. "Did you see it already, Hana?"

"Yeah, a newspaper-club member gave me a copy and said to pass it on to the clan head."

Nozomu's picture was splashed across the page. For a newspaper produced by a high school club, it looked quite professional. Hana was impressed. Saku would probably be happy when she showed it to him.

Maybe she should show it to Mio first, though.

Mio didn't seem like the type to lavish praise on her children, but even she should be able to find a congratulatory word or two after reading the heroic portrayal of her son written in the article.

As Hana perused the page, Suzu tapped her on the shoulder. "Hana, Hana."

"What?" she asked.

"She's back again."

"Hmm?"

Looming at their classroom door and staring at Hana—as usual—was Kikiyo.

However, there was something about the girl that was different.

She was laser focused on Hana, sure, but instead of her usual resentful glare, she was watching Hana with the forlorn eyes of an abandoned puppy.

Hana's words from the previous day must have struck a chord.

Hana assumed Kikiyo was going to gawk at her until the break was over, but after a short while, the other girl left the classroom. Up until now, she had refused to budge a single finger until the bell rang.

Hana was relieved that Kikiyo seemed to have finally given up her crusade. But she relaxed too soon. At lunch, Hana was eating with Suzu in the cafeteria when Kikiyo sat down quietly next to her.

Both Hana and Suzu looked surprised, their chopsticks pausing in midair.

Kiriya sat down across from his twin.

Hana turned a suspicious gaze on Kikiyo and said, "…What?"

"What do you mean?" the other girl asked.

"I mean, what are you sitting here for?"

"I'm free to sit wherever I like." Kikiyo's words were cool and collected, but she seemed on edge.

Hana felt rather than saw the girl's eyes flick toward her, sizing her up. She looked like she was itching to talk about something. Ignoring her was an option, but instead, Hana broke the ice first. "If you have something to say, just say it."

Kikiyo jumped, her gaze wandering until she seemed to seize her courage and opened her mouth to say, "I-I'm sorry…"

Hana was startled by the unexpected apology. "What for, all of a sudden?"

"For trying to force you to fight. It's just like you said. I disdain every girl who has anything to do with Lord Ichinomiya!" she admitted.

Kikiyo had finally taken off her mask and revealed her true self. Hana didn't scorn her for it but admired her instead.

"I've always looked up to Lord Ichinomiya," Kikiyo continued. "He's a wonderful practitioner and a wonderful man. I knew he wouldn't be able to avoid marriage if he became the head of the clan. So I begged my grandfather. I asked him to arrange for me to marry Lord Ichinomiya."

"What? Really?" Hana hadn't imagined Kikiyo would take things *that* far.

"But Grandfather stopped me from talking to Lord Ichinomiya. He said I was no good, that I wasn't Lord Ichinomiya's equal in terms of power... As his wife, I'm sure you know what I'm talking about."

"Hmm? Ohhh, right."

In order to strengthen the pillar's barrier, Saku's spouse had to be as strong as he was. As far as Hana could tell, the gap between Kikiyo and Saku was too large. Such a gulf would only get in Saku's way as he repaired the barrier.

The marriages of the lords of the five clans weren't built on love.

"When I heard Lord Ichinomiya was getting married, I thought his partner was going to be an extremely powerful woman. I kept wondering and wondering about what kind of person she was. So I had you investigated," Kikiyo said.

Her tone was nonchalant, not at all as if she'd just confessed to something horrifying. However, she didn't seem to see the problem.

It wasn't welcome news to hear that one's life had been pried into on the sly.

Oblivious to Hana's complex emotions, Kikiyo pressed forward with her explanation. "Then I found out that the one Lord Ichinomiya had picked wasn't the famously accomplished Hazuki but her *in*famously worthless twin sister."

As always, the girl looked like she was desperately holding back the tears threatening to spill from her eyes. Kiriya stroked her head comfortingly. "Don't cry," he said.

"Not crying yet, though," she said.

They really were a close pair of twins.

Between them was a bond built from mutual trust.

Every time she looked at Kikiyo and Kiriya, twins just like her, she couldn't help thinking about pointless things she couldn't change one way or another. Things like if she and Hazuki had such a close-knit relationship, maybe their situation would have turned out differently.

"I don't understand why a bottom-of-the-barrel practitioner like you was good enough to be the clan lord's bride and I wasn't," Kikiyo said. "I was sure you had gotten a hold of Lord Ichinomiya's weakness."

"If anything, it's the opposite," Hana grumbled.

"Really?"

"Well, it's something like that."

Hana had been hypnotized by money.

"…So that's why you agreed so quickly when I told you to get a divorce all of a sudden." Kikiyo put together the pieces. "Your willingness to sign the papers made me wonder all the more why you became Lord Ichinomiya's partner."

"And that's why you harassed me?"

"Harassed?!" Kikiyo blurted out. She looked astonished.

But if that wasn't harassment, what was? Hana was surprised Kikiyo had fooled herself into thinking otherwise.

"Nnngh, I have no defense, but I just— I needed to know why, no matter what. Why did Lord Ichinomiya pick you? Why not me?"

"Well, if there's a reason, it's because he's the lord of the clan, I suppose," replied Hana. "He needed my power. That's all."

"But you have no talent to speak of. Isn't that just your arrogance as his wife speaking?!" Tears began to fall from Kikiyo's eyes for real. She laid her face on the table.

Hana looked at the prone Kikiyo with helpless exasperation, and then she looked at the clock. It was almost time for the bell to ring.

Almost no other students were left in the cafeteria. The few remaining ones were on their way out. The only people still lounging about were Hana's group.

"Suzu, go to class without me," Hana said.

"What about you?" Suzu asked.

"Well, I can't just leave her like this, can I?" She glanced at Kikiyo, who was sniffling and crying like a child. She shot Suzu a rueful smile.

Suzu smiled back wearily. "That's true. I'll find an excuse to tell the teacher."

"Okay, thanks." Hana waved at Suzu as she left.

With the cafeteria now deserted, she mumbled, "Expand," conjuring a barrier of concealment. No one outside would be able to see the three of them, and their powers would be contained within.

Both Kikiyo, her cheeks wet with tears, and Kiriya were stunned by the sudden appearance of the barrier.

"Why did you place a barrier?" Kikiyo asked, question marks dancing above her head.

"Because I don't want anyone to see what I'm about to do." Hana grinned impishly at the other girl. She called the names of her hidden shikigami. "Aoi. Miyabi." The two shikigami materialized instantly.

Kikiyo's eyes widened into saucers at the appearance of the human shikigami. Even Kiriya was making an openly shocked expression; it was a satisfying sight to see.

"Um, Hana, who are they?" Kikiyo managed to ask.

"My shikigami, Aoi and Miyabi," Hana answered.

Miyabi smiled and bowed elegantly.

Aoi wore a haughty expression and didn't deign to greet the twins.

Kikiyo blurted out, "But they have human forms?!"

"Yup."

"You have two human shikigami?"

"Yup. That's why I was chosen," Hana said. "Because I'm strong enough to rival Saku."

Kikiyo looked between Miyabi and Aoi in disbelief, but after a second, she recovered her cool, and her expression became accepting. "So that's how it is… We were on different pages from the start. Why are you hiding this from everyone? No one would be able to call you worthless once they knew you had two human shikigami."

"Probably not. But in exchange, I'd have to give up my peaceful life. Frankly, I'm not ready for that yet," Hana replied.

Saku had warned her before.

It was impossible to hide forever, he had said.

Hana had a faint premonition of that herself, that the day would come when her powers were exposed to the world.

How would Hazuki and her parents react then?

Whatever happened, it was sure to be a headache.

That was why she planned to stand her ground until the very last moment.

"Anyway, setting that aside, do you get why Saku chose me now?" Hana asked.

Kikiyo looked shakily back at Miyabi and Aoi and smiled wistfully. "I think I do. I'm no match for you. I don't have the kind of overwhelming power needed to win over Lord Ichinomiya." She bowed deeply toward Hana. "I apologize for all the trouble I've caused you up until now. I will stop trying to put you to the test."

"That'd be great." That was the whole reason she'd undergone the risk of having Miyabi and Aoi manifest on school grounds.

"I have one more request," Kikiyo said.

"What is it?"

"Will you allow me to continue harassing you," Kikiyo asked, "but as a friend this time?" She peered up at Hana through her lashes, searching Hana's expression with anxiety in her eyes.

Hana smiled and stuck out her hand. "I don't care to be harassed, but… if it's as a friend."

Kikiyo brightened up. She looked happy as she grabbed Hana's hand.

Hana dismissed Aoi and Miyabi and released her barrier.

Class had started ages ago. A teacher was bound to come patrolling if they kept dawdling in the cafeteria. They decided to return to their respective classrooms.

Hana started to follow the chipper Kikiyo out of the cafeteria when Kiriya tapped her on the shoulder. She stopped. "What?"

"My sister has her faults, but I leave her in your hands," the boy said, as if he were giving away his daughter's hand in marriage, and bowed his head low.

"I'm not taking her as my bride," Hana retorted instinctively. She hoped he'd overlook the sass.

"Did I say something wrong?" he asked, perplexed.

"Many things."

Kiriya didn't seem to think there was anything unusual about what he had just said. He tilted his head questioningly as he went after Kikiyo.

"That boy really is a black box."

The entity called Kiriya and what he was remained the only open mystery.

Chapter 4

For several days after Hana agreed to be Kikiyo's friend, Kikiyo started dropping by Class C practically every hour to see Hana. The frequency of her visits wasn't new, but her attitude certainly was.

"Hanaaa!" Kikiyo looked like a puppy greeting her master with its tail wagging, openly ecstatic.

Before, she used to linger at the door, but she now regularly came into the classroom.

Of course, her twin, Kiriya, tagged along as well.

Hana's hands were full with studying for the upcoming exams, and she began to wonder if she should cut off the budding friendship while it was still early.

"Stop hounding me, I'm begging you," Hana said. "All the info I just finished shoving into my brain has flown right out the window…"

"You don't need to study so seriously. Talk to me instead." Kikiyo clung to Hana with a happy smile.

One person looked on jealously.

That person was the one acknowledged by all as Hana's best friend: Suzu.

"Hana's going to talk with me," Suzu snarled. "Go back to your own classroom and make friends with the Class A students!"

When the twins of the Nijouin main family had first transferred, Suzu had been beside herself with excitement, but with Kikiyo buddying up to Hana, the flames of hostility burned in her heart.

"I want to get to know Hana better," Kikiyo declared.

"Oh yeah? If so, you should go through her one and only best friend: me," Suzu huffed.

"Best friend?! I'm so jealous," Kikiyo whined. "I want to be her best friend, too! Can I, Hana?"

"No. Absolutely not! Hana's best friend is me! Right, Hana?!" Suzu demanded.

"Hmmm, I guess, yeah," Hana said. She had only just patched things up with Kikiyo, so the other girl couldn't be counted as a best friend.

Suzu rejoiced. "Yaaay!"

Kikiyo was dismayed. "No way!"

"Please, *please* be quiet already," Hana begged. She wasn't absorbing anything from the textbook. The other two were too noisy.

She felt the impending doom of Mio's special tutoring sessions and shuddered.

That was the one thing she had to avoid at all costs.

Hana stared at the twins. "Say, Kikiyo, Kiriya, you two are in Class A, yeah?" They were on a first-name basis now that they were friends.

"Yes. What of it?" Kikiyo asked.

"How good are your grades?"

"Let's see. Hazuki is number one in the practicals, followed by Nozomu, and then the two of us. In our lecture classes, Kiriya's beaten out Hazuki for the top spot."

"Huh, his grades are *that* good?"

"Kiriya's smart. My little brother is my pride and joy," Kikiyo boasted, her expression smug, as if it was her own grades she was talking about.

Hana hadn't found out that Kikiyo was the older of the twins until they'd become friends. When she heard, she had refrained from saying she had been positive it was the opposite. Kiriya was the more composed of the two and seemed older. Who would've thought he was actually the younger one?

"By the way, what about your grades?" Hana asked Kikiyo.

Kikiyo looked away. That reaction was enough to give away exactly how she scored on her tests. For some reason, Suzu suddenly smiled kindly and patted Kikiyo's shoulder.

Their grades may have been equally bad, but Class A and C were as different as heaven and earth. Hana neglected to point that out.

◆

Hana's school life had, on the whole, become lively.

The terrorists were still on the loose, but her days passed peacefully.

Then one day, a familiar face visited the Ichinomiya residence.

Hana was studying furiously in her room when Towa announced, "Madam, you have a guest. What would you like to do?"

"A guest? Who is it?" Hana asked.

This was the first time anyone had come to see her there. Saku had barred her parents from meeting with her, and it was a tall order for Suzu, part of a Sankourou branch family, to come calling at the main Ichinomiya house.

Hana couldn't think of any other potential visitors. She tilted her head, puzzled.

"The guest called herself 'Sae,'" Towa said.

"Oh! Sae?!" Hana gasped. She scrambled to ask Towa to show Sae to the reception room, then she straightened up her appearance and went to meet with her former servant.

She hadn't seen Sae since she'd left the Ichise household. Her heart beat rapidly as she stepped inside the room. There, waiting for her, was the same Sae she'd always known.

"Miss Hana!" Sae cried, overcome with emotion. Her voice was rough with tears. She turned to face Hana, and without rising from her formal kneeling seat, she bowed her head.

Hana rushed to the woman. "It's been so long, Sae."

Sae raised her head and looked at Hana. "It feels like we haven't met in years."

"It really does. I'm sorry I didn't get to say thank you or good-bye before I left the house, Sae."

"Please do not worry yourself," Sae said. "Are you happy living here, Miss Hana? You no longer have to endure the kinds of hardships you underwent in the Ichise household?"

"I'm fine. Saku, his mother, and the staff are good to me," Hana reassured her.

"I'm glad to hear that." A warm, maternal smile rose to Sae's face. She looked genuinely happy for Hana.

Indeed, Sae was more of a mother to Hana than her flesh-and-blood mother was.

"So why are you here?" Hana asked. "I was surprised to hear you were visiting all of a sudden."

She'd had the room cleared, so she and Sae were alone.

In fact, Aoi and Miyabi were standing behind Hana, too, but unlike Saku, who could pinpoint exactly where the two were, Sae didn't sense a thing, for she had little talent as a practitioner.

Arashi was napping in the hallway that wrapped around the house, visible for all to behold. There wasn't anyone foolish enough in the household to lay their hands on a god; unlike the average joe on the street, they all knew exactly how fearsome a god could be. Arashi lazed around where he pleased without having to watch his back.

Sae's face had clouded over the moment Hana asked the reason for her visit. She bowed her head low, her forehead kissing the tatami mat. "Please save Miss Hazuki!" she begged.

Surprise flashed across Hana's face before her expression became hawkish. "What are you talking about?"

"I know that I'm overstepping my bounds as a servant," Sae said, "but the master and mistress are completely disregarding the young miss's wishes... I can't bear to see her so defeated."

Hana tamped down on her instinct to yell and bombard Sae with questions. She reined in her emotions and asked, "What happened?"

It must've been something major for Sae to visit her, and whatever it was, she sensed it was connected to the earlier incident when Hazuki had lost control of her powers.

Sae explained, "The master intends to marry off Miss Hazuki. Her husband has already been selected."

"What?"

"The groom is from a branch family and is over twenty years her senior. It appears that the master plans to use the marriage to dramatically raise the family's influence within the clan."

"...That scumbag of a father," Hana spat venomously. "Don't tell me Hazuki agreed to it."

"It is as you fear," Sae replied. "No, Miss Hazuki never had the right to refuse in the first place. You know well that the master is not the kind of person who would give up when told 'no.'"

"Yes, I know. But even so, how could they ignore Hazuki's feelings in such an important decision?"

Alas, the signs had been there all along.

When Saku had been selecting his bride, hadn't they pressured Hazuki to win his hand no matter the cost?

Those two saw their daughter as nothing more than a tool, and marriage was simply a way to improve the family's standing. Love wasn't part of the discussion.

"How long will they keep using Hazuki before they're satisfied?" Rage welled up within Hana. She was so furious, the thought of calling those people her mother and father disgusted her. "But Hazuki's at fault, too. If she doesn't want to, she should put her foot down. She's playing the role of the perfect, understanding daughter as always. To some extent, she's reaping exactly what she sowed."

If Hazuki had something to say, all she had to do was speak, instead of bottling everything up inside.

And yet she never said anything.

She was a mute puppet under their parents' control.

"You're wrong, Miss Hana," Sae said. "You've misunderstood your sister."

"How so?"

"Miss Hazuki bade me to keep quiet, but her order is surely invalid at this point. She has always tried to protect you, Miss Hana, but as things stand, she will never be happy again."

"...What do you mean, 'protect'?"

Protect Hana?

What could Sae possibly be talking about?

Hana's face stiffened.

"Miss Hana complies with your parents' will in order to protect you," Sae declared.

"I don't understand!" yelled Hana, her voice trembling.

Sae just looked at her with a strong and steady gaze. Those unflinching eyes prompted Hana to regain her composure.

Sae opened her mouth to speak. "The master and mistress have always treated you coldly, believing you were untalented and worthless. However, their attitude toward you took a sharp turn for the worse after you conjured your shikigami."

"...That's right." Hana had been overjoyed to have her first shikigami, naturally, but her parents had seen Azuha as garbage.

Hana would never forget the look in her parents' eyes at that moment.

"The shikigami you called forth was an insect, the weakest of all forms. The master despaired of that result. That's when they started to discuss putting you up for adoption so that you wouldn't shackle down the Ichise family."

"What?!" Hana cried. It was her first time hearing this.

But she couldn't deny that her parents would stoop to such lengths. The thought made her terribly sad.

"The one who put a stop to it was Miss Hazuki. She pleaded with the master and mistress to let you stay. In exchange, she said she would work hard enough for both of you."

Hana felt as if she'd been punched in the head. "...I didn't know that..."

"As you are aware, after that, the master and mistress hired tutors for her and imposed on her a thoroughly unreasonable workload," Sae continued. "And as she promised, she excelled in all her subjects, never uttering a word of complaint."

"...You've known this all along, Sae?"

"No, I, too, found out only recently. When the servant assigned to Miss Hazuki quit, she told me everything. She said that as things are, Miss Hazuki is too pitiful."

Hana's thoughts were a jumbled mess.

Deep down, she had always thought of herself as the victim and her family as the perpetrators.

But that may not have been the case.

At the very least, Hazuki had apparently sacrificed herself for Hana's sake.

Hana's expression was miserable—as if she'd burst into tears any second. She looked at Sae imploringly. "Sae..."

Sae came up to Hana quietly and took her hand. "Miss Hana. Please save Miss Hazuki. I want to see the two of you friendly again, the way you were in the past."

"Even if you tell me that, Hazuki's not going to listen to anything I say."

That was the way it had always been.

You're too stupid to understand, she would say and fling away Hana's hand.

What was Hana supposed to say in the face of such hostility?

Seeing Hana balk, Sae chided her, "Do not be afraid, Miss Hana. No matter how fiercely she resists, the only one who can reach her is you. That's because of the strong bond between the two of you."

"Hazuki and I have nothing to do with each other."

That bond had been severed long ago.

The kind of trust shared between Kikiyo and Kiriya didn't exist between her and Hazuki.

"No," Sae said, "you are still connected. You simply have not noticed. Miss Hazuki is waiting for you."

Hana's usual mettle was nowhere to be seen. She was like a lost child who didn't know where to go.

Then...Aoi and Miyabi showed themselves.

"Master," Aoi said.

"Master Hana," said Miyabi.

Sae was shocked into silence.

"Go, Master," Aoi said.

"But Hazuki won't listen to a word I say. What am I supposed to do?" Hana asked.

"Reveal your powers. You don't need to be protected anymore. Show that girl you have the strength to be the protector," Aoi told her.

Miyabi added, "If there is still hope of repairing your relationship, you must do all you can. You can't leave Hazuki be. That much is written plainly on your face. Why not try everything you can?"

"That might mean the loss of the peaceful life you want. Which is more important to you? That girl or your days of peace and quiet?" Aoi asked.

"I don't…" Hana trailed off.

There was no need to think. The answer was obvious.

At that moment, a brilliant light flared to life in Hana's eyes.

"And that's why you're our master," said Aoi.

"Call for us any time you're in need of our power. We are always on your side, Master," Miyabi reassured her.

With those words, the two shikigami vanished.

"Ahhh, Miss Hana. The lady and gentleman from a second ago, are they shikigami?" Sae asked.

"Mm-hmm, yeah," Hana replied.

"They called you 'Master.'" Sae looked bewildered. That was only natural. In the Ichise household, Hana was known as a good-for-nothing.

But those days might be at an end.

She didn't want to make the wrong choice of what to protect.

"Sae, I'm going to write Hazuki a letter," Hana said. "Can you give it to her without letting my parents see?"

"You wish to keep it a secret from the master and mistress?"

Judging from Sae's troubled expression, she was asking for the impossible.

Hazuki's schedule was planned down to the minute, and she hardly ever had a moment alone in the house. The only time she was alone was when she was sleeping.

In that case, it might be easier to talk to her at school. But Hana would attract attention if she was to call Hazuki out.

Then she'd just have to ask Kikiyo, who was in Hazuki's class.

Nozomu was an option, too.

As she was agonizing over what to do…

"Your letter, I'll deliver it," said an unfamiliar, childlike voice.

Hana whirled around and saw Hiragi, Hazuki's shikigami.

"You're… What are you doing here?" Hana asked.

"I followed her," Hiragi said and pointed at Sae.

Sae looked surprised. It seemed that she hadn't known. "My word… I didn't notice at all."

"Shikigami are hard to detect when they've hidden themselves, unless your senses are exceptionally sharp," Hana explained.

Someone with Saku's ability might realize, but Hana hadn't picked up on anything, either. She was a powerful practitioner, but she wasn't as perceptive as Saku was.

"More importantly, you said you're going to pass on my letter?" asked Hana.

"That's right. *I* can meet with Hazuki without raising suspicion," Hiragi said.

"That's true…" But Hana was torn as to whether she could believe him.

Everything would be over if her letter ended up in someone else's hands.

Asking Kikiyo might be the safer option.

That was when Hiragi dropped down to his knees, sitting formally. Perhaps he had noticed Hana's internal conflict. "I want to save Hazuki, too," he said. "If that is your goal, I will lend you a hand. Shikigami that

I am, I can't defy Hazuki's orders, so I need your help. Please." He bowed his head low.

Hana decided then and there that Hiragi was trustworthy.

His sincerity had reminded her of something.

He reminded Hana of Aoi and Miyabi when they were acting on her behalf.

"Okay. You must give it to her without anyone seeing," she urged.

"Understood," Hiragi said.

And so Hana entrusted Hiragi with the letter.

◆

The next day, Hana went up to the school roof. Looking down through the fence, she could see the entire grounds. She watched the kids in gym class as she waited.

The door to the roof opened, and Hazuki stepped out. There was a hint of rigidity in her expression.

Hana turned around slowly. "Hazuki…"

"Hana…," Hazuki said.

Their gazes locked, each looking at the other girl whose face was a mirror image of her own.

Hazuki was the first to turn away.

"What do you want? Using Hiragi to send me a letter… What were you thinking?" Hazuki demanded.

"…Yesterday, Sae came to visit me," Hana said.

"She did?"

Sae had mostly taken care of Hana and had had little contact with Hazuki. Nonetheless, Hazuki was aware of who she was.

"Is it true? That you're getting married?"

Hazuki swallowed thickly. But a moment later, anger bled into her expression. "Did you hear that from Sae? Or was it Hiragi?"

"Who cares how I found out? Are you seriously going to marry someone you don't know the first thing about?"

"It's none of your business! You have nothing to do with the Ichise family anymore."

"I do!" Hana grabbed Hazuki by the arm and fixed her with a piercing stare. "We're twins. Can't I worry about my other half?"

"Other half...? You're saying that now?! When you've been scornful all this time?! Weren't you the one who threw us away and ran off to the Ichinomiyas?"

"The Ichises were the ones who forced my hand, right? No, I should say that it was our parents. They were the ones to poison the well."

Hana had never openly criticized their parents before, and Hazuki looked shocked. "How can you talk about Mother and Father that way?"

"Those sorry excuses for parents think we're nothing more than tools! That includes you, Hazuki. For the sake of the family, for the Ichise bloodline, they'll wring you dry."

"It's not like that!" Hazuki yelled.

"It's exactly like that!" Hana shouted over Hazuki, refuting her protest. "Do you remember what I said the day I left the house? That you never do anything for yourself? I must apologize to you. I'm sorry." Hana bowed deeply, regretful that she had forced Hazuki to bear the burden alone the whole time.

Hazuki was shaken by Hana's apology. "What are you trying to pull all of a sudden...?"

"Sae told me everything. She told me you negotiated with our parents to protect me when they tried to abandon me."

Hazuki was speechless. Her eyes were wide.

"I always thought you were an idiot for doing everything our parents said. You never say anything selfish and never try to resist. I thought you were like a doll—that you would lose everything that makes you *you*. And when you ignored my warnings over and over, I deserted you. That's why I want to apologize."

"..."

"Everything you did was for my sake, but I didn't realize a thing and just did whatever I wanted. I'm really sorry," Hana said. "But it's okay now."

"What is…?"

"You don't need to protect me anymore. I can manage myself. You can be free, Hazuki. From me, from our parents, from the Ichise family."

Hana took one step forward. Hazuki took one step back.

"That's impossible," Hazuki said. "Mother and Father would never allow that…"

"Well then, you're going to end up married to some guy twenty years older than you. Are you seriously okay with that?!"

"O-of course not! I don't want that at all!" Hazuki shouted, her voice trembling. But her next words were unsure and came out in a whisper. "But I can't go against our parents."

"You're going to keep doing what they want for the rest of your life? If you throw away your own heart, what are you going to have left in the end?"

"I don't know! But it doesn't matter even if I say no. They're never going to listen to me."

"You won't know that until you try!" Hana squeezed Hazuki's shoulder roughly and shook her.

As if by doing so, she could wake Hazuki up.

"You've never once tried to defy them, so why have you already decided it's useless? You have to at least try."

"You can only say such carefree things because you don't know anything. Mother and Father only care about the family. They won't listen to me."

"Then dump them!" Hana yelled. Hazuki's eyes widened. "Father, Mother, the whole Ichise family, all the pains-in-the-neck—you can just ditch them all. That's what I did. I was going to throw you away with the rest, but I take it back. Let's both rid ourselves of the Ichises." She grinned impishly.

Hazuki was deeply shaken by Hana's speech. She snarled back furiously, "Wha—?! Do you hear how ridiculous you sound? You're being too selfish! You already tossed me aside. Now leave me alone."

"No. Way! I'll be as selfish as I like, thank you very much. I already decided I'm gonna live the way I want, without the Ichises or our stupid father interfering. And I'm taking you along with me," Hana declared.

"To where?! What are you planning?!"

"Did you forget who I am? I'm the wife of the Ichinomiya lord. I have way more influence now than Father and the others. I may be masquerading as Lady Ichinomiya, but I'm going to milk this borrowed authority to crush the Ichises. Just you watch, you shitty old man. Heh-heh-heh."

Hazuki flinched at the wicked expression on Hana's face and her dark chuckle. "Were you always this crooked?"

Hana turned away, her expression stony. "It's not my fault. This is the handiwork of our fool of a father and his followers." She turned to face Hazuki again and offered her hand, hoping fervently for Hazuki to take it. "The rest is up to you. What do you want to do, Hazuki?"

Hana's hand quivered so minutely, her sister wouldn't notice.

She was scared, too. Scared that the olive branch she'd offered without thinking about the consequences would be knocked away. "Hazuki," she implored.

"Ah...I..."

Hana could see Hazuki's inner turmoil. It couldn't have been easy for her to be told out of the blue to throw away her family.

But Hazuki was almost out of time.

Once the parents of the two households officially met, they would undoubtedly wish to marry Hazuki off as quickly as possible.

Hana tried again. "Hazuki, please."

Forget the Ichises' happiness. Choose your own happiness, she begged.

At that moment, a small shade passed in front of the twins.

Hana was blindsided by the shade's sudden appearance, but she wasn't the only one. Hazuki also looked at it with surprise.

Then multiple screams erupted from the schoolyard below. The two of them whipped their heads over to peer down past the fence and were flabbergasted at what they found.

"What…the hell…?" Hana mumbled.

A whole slew of shades, too many to count, had appeared out of nowhere and were attacking the students.

Shrieks were coming from every direction and echoed through the yard. The students ran around in a panic.

But that wasn't all.

Large numbers of shades had swarmed around Hana and Hazuki as well.

"Expand!" Hana yelled, throwing a barrier around their surroundings.

Hazuki called out, "Hiragi!" summoning her shikigami in alarm.

He manifested instantly and began to take out the shades with sweeps of a fanlike tool.

"Eliminate!" Hana roared, burning to destroy the shades around her. But her abilities had no effect. "What?! Why isn't it working?!"

"Hana, get back!" Hazuki shouted. "They're extremely strong."

Hana inspected the shades more thoroughly. Like Hazuki had said, they were terrifyingly powerful.

She realized that with her powers dampened as they usually were, she wouldn't be able to kill the shades.

"So that's how it's going to be. Expand!" Given the size of the swarm, Hana didn't have the luxury to be holding back. She gave up on her restrictions and threw everything she had at the onslaught. "Eliminate!"

Crack! Crack! Crack! Crack! Her one attack decimated a swath of shades.

Hazuki watched in astonishment. "Just now, did *you* do that? But you're supposed to be weak…"

"I'll explain later. First, we have to take care of the shades in the school somehow. I'm going to call Saku, so keep an eye out for me."

"I—I got it."

Hazuki wasted no time on pointless arguing and focused instead on what needed to be done. As expected of a top student in Class A.

Hana laughed weakly and took out her phone to make the call.

But there was no signal.

"It won't connect!" Hana cried.

Hazuki had been looking down at the schoolyard, but she whirled around. "What? Why?"

"Is your phone working?"

"Wait a second…" She fished her phone from her pocket to check. "…No, I'm also out of range." It was useless, too.

Hana had been in a similar situation before.

She peered into the distance, squinting in concentration. There was a distortion in the boundary between the school and the outside world. She spun around, scanning their surroundings as Hazuki looked on quizzically.

"What are you doing, Hana?" Hazuki asked.

"There's a barrier around the school grounds," explained Hana. "That's why there's no signal."

"What?!" Hazuki turned toward where Hana was looking and strained her eyes to search for signs of such a barrier. In the end, she cocked her head in confusion. Apparently, she hadn't been able to see anything. "What are you talking about? Where?" she asked.

"Over there. Right between the school wall and the grounds."

"I don't see anything."

"I didn't notice it going up at all. Azuha, do you think you can cross through it?" Hana asked the shikigami who'd flown off her hair and was now perching on her finger.

Azuha paused before answering, "Yes, I think so."

"Can you go get Saku, then?"

"Yes, Master." She fluttered off, pausing briefly at the rippling in the air Hana had seen, before continuing through it.

Hana observed the shades' movements. She concluded that they couldn't go past the barrier.

That wasn't all. When the students tried to escape outside, they, too, were prevented from leaving the grounds.

In other words, the school had become a giant cage packed with shades.

If shades this powerful couldn't leave, then most of the people trapped inside had no hope of getting out, either.

"Hazuki, let's head back in for now and help the others evacuate," Hana declared. "Class A students have experience rooting out shades, so maybe they can take care of themselves, but there's just too many shades. Some of them must have also gotten inside the building."

"Right. But evacuate to where? It doesn't look like leaving is going to be an option," Hazuki said.

"A barrier of that level…I can just punch through it."

Azuha had been able to leave, so Hana figured that she should be able to as well.

Hana continued, "With all the teachers and the Class A kids' power combined, they should be able to put up barriers to protect everyone at least temporarily, right?"

"Probably, but what do you plan to do after that?" Hazuki asked. "If we follow your suggestion and break through the barrier, the shades will be able to escape too, and we'd end up putting regular people in danger."

"That's exactly why I sent Azuha to get Saku. With Saku around, everything will work out one way or another."

"But—"

"We don't have time to stand around talking. People are going to die if we don't act now!"

Nozomu, Kikiyo, and Kiriya were in the same class as Hazuki. Their class was levels above the first- and second-year Class As.

Hana told Hazuki to get to the front gate and set up a barrier there as well if they had the people and energy to spare. That way, the students in the yard would have a safe place to hide.

Browbeaten by Hana, Hazuki reluctantly ran off to her class.

Hana went inside, exterminating shades as she went. In an offshoot of the hallway, she summoned Aoi and Miyabi. They answered her call and appeared with worried expressions.

"Aoi, you go lead the Class C students still left in the classroom to the front gate," Hana ordered. "I'm going to the broadcasting room. If you run into anyone else who was slow to run, take them with you."

"What about you, Master?" Aoi asked.

"I'll be fine. Miyabi, I'm counting on you to take care of the students out on the grounds."

"Understood," Miyabi said.

"Go. Suzu should be in the classroom, too. You must protect her."

Aoi and Miyabi both bowed and quickly vanished.

Hana had no time to stand around, either.

"Ahhh, god, give me a break. What a pain in the neck. Why'd this have to happen now?!"

She turned a corner and ran headfirst into a shade. She annihilated it on sight and continued on toward the broadcasting room.

She arrived at her destination to find several teachers crowded around the mic, frantically trying to explain the situation.

"Please let me through!" Hana said.

"Wait, hey! What do you think you're doing?"

She ignored them and grabbed the mic. "Hello, hello. Testing, one, two, three. All students in the building should make their way to Class A or the teachers' room. Teachers, Class A students, and anyone else skilled at barrier work, please erect barriers in those locations to serve as temporary shelters. To anyone powerless to help, get to a shelter and *behave*. Word has been sent to the head of the Ichinomiya clan. The Association of Practitioners will soon provide help!"

After spewing out her speech in one go, she took a deep breath and turned to face the teachers again.

"Was that true?" one asked. "You were able to contact the Ichinomiya clan head?"

"Judging by your surprise, I'm guessing your phones aren't connecting, either?" Hana asked.

"Yes. But that aside, you've got some nerve barging in here all of a sudden!"

Hana didn't want to hear that from the chumps who'd been running around like chickens with their heads cut off.

"If you have the time to fuss over trivial details, go gather the students still stuck in the building and help put up the barriers already!" Hana demanded. "Do you want people to die?!"

The teachers flinched back from the threat in Hana's eyes, and she forcibly expelled them from the room.

After repeating the explanation she'd given one more time, she turned her energy toward slaughtering the shades that had infiltrated the school.

But there were just too many.

"I should've brought Arashi!" she complained.

The inugami would've run a circle through the building, clearing out the shades effortlessly as he went.

It was frustrating to picture him lounging around the Ichinomiya residence, taking a nap, which was likely exactly what he was doing.

Nearly an hour must've passed since Hana had sent Azuha after Saku.

While Hana was single-mindedly massacring every shade in sight, a voice called her from behind.

"Master."

Hana proffered her finger to Azuha, who was flittering toward her.

"Where's Saku?" she asked.

"Outside the front gate. He's waiting for you."

"Got it. Thanks, Azuha."

Azuha lifted off again and returned to her perch in Hana's hair.

"I ought to hurry if he's already here." Hana changed directions and broke out into a run, heading for the school entrance.

In front of the gate, students from Hazuki's class had erected a barrier, inside which they were enduring the onslaught while protecting the students who had been stranded on the grounds.

Aoi and Miyabi were next to them, felling the shades nearby.

Without calling out to her shikigami, Hana pushed her way through the other students to the boundary of the barrier cutting the school off from outside.

On the other side was Saku and several practitioners.

"Are you all right, Hana?" Saku asked.

"I'm dizzy from killing too many of the damned things," she said, shrugging. She looked like she still had plenty of energy to spare. "I've changed my mind about the shades in the villa. They were rather cute now that I'm thinking about it."

"Look at you so chipper. I needn't have worried," Saku said. "Can you break the barrier from your side? Unfortunately, I didn't bring anyone strong enough to deal with it. I'll replace it with a new one the moment it's down to prevent the shades from escaping."

"Okay." Hana turned to the nearby students. "You there, make some space."

She waved the other students back, but they didn't want to follow her orders.

"What're you acting so high-and-mighty for, Class C trash?"

"Leftover scraps should know when to shut their traps. What can you even do?"

To muzzle the idiots who were gibbering away when every second was a battle for their lives, Hana sucked in a huge breath and bellowed, "Shut up! Stop your whining and get out of the way already! Otherwise, I'm gonna toss you out and let the shades have you!!"

Hana usually didn't respond to the insults hurled her way. The other students were stunned to see her yell.

While they were down for the count, Saku backed up Hana's offensive. "Are you deaf? *Move.* Don't you want to be rescued?"

"Eek! Yes, right away!"

Hana suspected they scrambled aside because they were afraid of Saku more so than her, but she dismissed the details for now.

She backed away into the newly opened space. Then she charged headlong into the barrier. As she neared it, without slowing her momentum, she launched into a flying kick.

There was a *crack!* like glass shattering. Simultaneously, Saku called out, "Bind!" his voice ringing around the yard.

The original barrier was broken. In its place was the barrier Saku conjured.

"Now everyone should be able to get out. All students who aren't practitioners should leave the grounds," Saku said.

The students took his cue and scrambled away from the school with the force of an avalanche.

"Thank god. We're finally out!"

"We're saved."

Surrounded by students, some of whom were crying, Hana made her way to Saku's side. "Hey, this has something to do with the Skull and Spider Lily, doesn't it?" she asked.

"Sharp," he said.

"I knew it…" Unfortunately, her bad premonition had been right on the mark. "Don't tell me, were they targeting me or Nozomu?"

"Or those two over there."

Hana traced Saku's gaze over to where Kikiyo and Kiriya were standing. The twins faced Saku and bowed politely.

Saku called over to them, "How does this look from the Nijouins' perspective?"

"It is possible that the Nijouin talismans were used to set all this up," Kikiyo answered firmly.

A confident smile rose to his face. "I agree. One to draw shades in and one to set up a barrier."

"Those kinds of talismans exist?" Hana asked.

"Yeah. A similar talisman to the latter—albeit a weaker counterpart—was used to create the barrier around the villa I gave you. They're not considered dangerous, so the perpetrators likely had one in their possession to begin with."

"I see."

Hana's intuition that the barriers around the villa and the school were similar had proved correct.

"But the talisman to summon shades is SS rank. Dangerous and deadly. I never imagined it would be used here. The one saving grace in this nightmare is that you were here, Hana. It seems that the Skull and Spider Lily hadn't accounted for your abilities in their calculations."

A disconcerting grin rose to Saku's face—*what's so funny?*—and he reached out to tousle Hana's hair.

"Hey!" she cried.

"I have to go inside to search for the talismans," Saku said. "Take over the barrier for me."

"Seriously? What a pain," she whined. She had been busy slaying scores of the shades up until a minute ago. What a slave driver.

"What do you want me to do? There's only two people here who can summon a barrier to cover the entire school: me and you."

"Uuugh." Hana's expression twisted in distaste, but Saku only looked at her demandingly.

As they were locked in their standoff, whispers rumbled through the crowd.

"There's no way in hell a good-for-nothing like her can do that."

"Right? All the Third Color teachers *combined* wouldn't be enough. It's impossible for her by herself."

"Hazuki's scraps…"

"Waste of air…"

The mutterings were all slander aimed at Hana. The malcontents were keeping their voices low because of Saku's presence, but they were still perfectly audible.

"Hana…," Hazuki said hesitantly. She was standing a distance away, looking at Hana with a worried expression.

Hana was going to free Hazuki from the Ichises.

She had resolved to do everything in her power to accomplish that. No one was coercing her. She'd made the decision herself.

"Fine, fine, I get it already." Hana folded to Saku's demand. "But hurry it up."

"I'll handle it," Saku said and patted her head, gently this time. Then he turned to Kikiyo and Kiriya. "I didn't want to involve students in this case, but I need your expertise as part of the Nijouin clan. It might be dangerous, but please come with me."

"We intended to do so from the beginning," Kikiyo said. Kiriya nodded beside her.

"Good," Saku said. "Hana, the barrier, if you'd please."

"Got it."

Hana made a frame with her fingers as if she was trying to find the best angle for a picture. She measured the size of the school and then stuck her hand out in front of her, fingers splayed. "Expand."

Her power manifested physically, laying a new barrier on top of Saku's.

The clamor broke out around them.

"No way. She really did it."

"Was she seriously the one who made that?"

"But she... I can't believe it..."

While exclamations of surprise poured out from the crowd, Saku dissolved his own barrier. Hana's work was solid. The shades remained trapped neatly inside. After making sure everything was squared away, Saku set out, bringing the twins with him. "Let's go."

Shades were still wandering around the grounds. It wasn't safe just yet. They had to rescue the people stuck within as quickly as possible.

"Aoi, Miyabi," Hana said, "we'll be fine out here. Go protect Kikiyo and Kiriya."

"You got it," Aoi said.

"Understood," Miyabi added.

Hearing Hana address Aoi and Miyabi, the people who'd been wondering all this time whom the two human shikigami belonged to stared at her agog.

Hana savored the fresh reactions of the crowd while feigning indifference. Inside, she was thinking that the news was going to blow up once the school reopened.

But now that she had revealed her hand, Hana would no longer need Hazuki's protection.

Hazuki approached her. Hana turned a luminous smile on her sister and said, "See, Hazuki? I'm strong, right? Stronger than you. You don't have to protect me anymore. From now on, let me protect you."

"Hana…" Tears slid quietly down Hazuki's cheeks, and she buried her face in Hana's shoulder.

This was the first time Hana had seen Hazuki cry.

The ones who'd driven Hazuki to this point were none other than their parents.

Hana had never felt so furious at them. She patted her sister's back softly as she fiercely tamped down on her nearly murderous wrath.

"You better believe I'm going to settle the score."

◆

The talismans used in the invasion on Obsidian High did indeed turn out to be the ones stolen from the Association. Once they were recovered on the grounds, they were swiftly returned to the headquarters.

Apparently, Kikiyo and Kiriya's transfer had also been motivated by the theft. The accomplices who had made it possible for the terrorists to infiltrate the headquarters in the first place were affiliated with the Nijouin clan.

The twins had been transferred to Obsidian High Campus One, located in the headquarters' territory, as representatives of their clan and to hunt for the missing talismans.

That information was undisclosed to the public since it could undermine trust in the five clans.

The reason Hana found out was because Saku had charged her with another impossible task.

"Really, again?" Hana grumbled.

"Yes. I need you to help resolve this incident," Saku said.

"What are you gonna give me this time?"

"You already got your villa, you gold digger."

"I'm just sooo unmotivated when there's no reward involved."

Saku shot a weary look at Hana, who was sprawled out lazily with her head pillowed on Arashi. Saku sighed in defeat. "What do you want?"

"Hmmm...what indeed? Another oceanside villa, for starters. A *proper* one this time," she demanded. "Furnishings and appliances to go with it. And a car. And a boat. And..."

"That's too much! You can have one thing. One."

"Boo. What to do...?" Hana was quiet for a moment, mulling things over. Then she slowly sat up. "Does it have to be something material?" Her face was serious, all traces of humor gone.

Saku composed himself. "Tell me what you're thinking."

So Hana did.

The corner of his lip curled upward, and he said, "Not bad."

◆

The school reopened after being shut down by the shade invasion.

To avoid being caught unaware by another attack, Hana decided to free Arashi from watch duty and bring him with her to school.

When Arashi heard the story, he said he would accompany her until the terrorist incident was settled, and she happily accepted.

However, upon arriving at school, she immediately realized she'd made a mistake.

Hana normally inhibited her powers, so most practitioners would see her as weak and talentless.

But Arashi was not just a shikigami. He was a proper god.

The divine power emanating from his being could only be tamped down to an extent.

Even the students, inexperienced as they were, could tell he was no ordinary shikigami.

"Wow, that shikigami's not like the others, is it?"

"Its power is on a whole 'nother level."

"The rumor must be true, that Hazuki's younger sister is actually an extraordinary practitioner."

"Then why is she in Class C?"

But Arashi wasn't all that was talked about.

"You said you saw her put up the barrier, right?"

"Yeah. It was amazing. There's no way your average practitioner could conjure a barrier *that* strong by themselves."

"I was there, too. Apparently, it wasn't a miracle that Lord Ichinomiya picked her after all."

"With her power, I wouldn't be surprised if he headhunted her himself. It looked like he trusts her, like they had each other's backs. They were so cool."

Hana buried her head in her hands in despair at the worshipful commentary. "It's worse than I imagined."

She'd known this would happen since she'd put on such a flagrant display of her powers, but it had blown into an even bigger topic than she'd predicted.

She got to her class to find her classmates dying to speak to her. However, it was hard for them to approach her with Arashi, who exuded an abnormal pressure, at her heels. They were torn by indecision.

Through the crowd of vultures came Suzu, wearing her usual smile. Her presence was a soothing balm for Hana's soul.

"Good morning, Hana."

"Suzu! You really are my angel," Hana said and hugged her friend tightly.

Judging from Suzu's expression, she didn't quite understand what was going on, but she seemed pleased nevertheless and returned the hug.

"You're amazing, Hana. You've become famous overnight! You're all anyone at school can talk about," Suzu said proudly, as if it were her own accomplishments she was speaking of.

Then she finally noticed Arashi sitting by Hana's feet. "Oh, this cutie must be the inugami from before. He's your shikigami now, I suppose." Even though Suzu had been attacked by Arashi when he was a tatarigami, she stroked his head without fear or hesitation. "Wow, he's like a cloud. I want a shikigami like him, too."

Suzu's squirrel shikigami was riding on her shoulder and pulled on her hair jealously.

How heartwarming.

Hana was truly thankful that she had a friend like Suzu who didn't treat her any differently despite everything that had happened.

On the other side of the spectrum...

"Wait. Isn't an inugami a god?"

"She has an actual god acting as her shikigami?"

"I don't know whether to be impressed or terrified."

"Seriously, what is she doing in Class C when she could easily be in Class A?"

The other students looked at Hana oddly or with downright suspicion.

The person they'd written off as deadweight could actually wield vast amounts of power.

Hana had realized there were bound to be people who'd react negatively, but the blatant rejections made her glum. She'd gotten along with her classmates until now, but all the students in Class C nursed an inferiority complex. Now that Hana had proved to be strong after all, the change didn't sit well with some people.

There wasn't anything she could do but ignore it.

Classes were conducted as usual. During the lunch break, instead of the usual Nijouin twins, Hana's other half, Hazuki, came calling.

Hazuki hardly ever stopped by Class C, so the surprised students stared at her curiously. Technically speaking, her visit shouldn't have been anything extraordinary given that her twin was in the class.

Hana stood up from her seat, bewildered, and went up to Hazuki. "Did you need something?" she asked.

"Are you free? I want to talk," Hazuki said. "About the disturbance with the shades...and about your powers."

"All right." Hana glanced at her usual lunch mate, Suzu, who waved her off with a smile that said, *Have fun!* She waved back, grateful that Suzu was so perceptive.

Hana followed Hazuki out of the classroom to the roof, where they'd spoken before. It was the most isolated place, hardly ever visited by other students, so they could talk freely.

"What do you want to know?" Hana asked.

"About your powers! Aren't you supposed to be weak? Your shikigami's a butterfly, isn't it? You shouldn't have been able to pull off any of what you did."

"You're not wrong," she said. Then she told Azuha, who was perched obediently in Hana's hair like a pretty clip, "You can stop suppressing your abilities, Azuha."

The butterfly shikigami fluttered between Hana and Hazuki and did as she had been instructed.

The moment she unleashed her powers, her wings took on a splendid rainbow hue. A palpable strength, one that could rival a human shikigami's, emanated from her.

It seemed that Hazuki had no problems sensing it, either. She looked astonished.

Hana followed up Azuha's demonstration with an explanation. "It's true. I used to be at the bottom of the barrel. My capabilities were a far cry from yours. That's why people called me your leftover scraps and said I was a good-for-nothing. Everything they said was right. I can't deny it."

"But you're actually unbelievably strong."

"On our fifteenth birthday, everything changed. Until then, my abilities were nothing to speak of, but suddenly, I awakened to massive amounts of latent power. It was like my weakness before had been a lie. I know it's hard to believe."

In fact, Hana had trouble believing it herself. She still had no idea what had triggered her transformation. The only thing she knew was that she had obtained powers that outstripped even Hazuki's that day.

"Why did you hide it?" Hazuki asked.

"Because it would've been a pain not to," Hana answered without hesitation. "What do you think would've happened if our parents had found out I had all this power? Obviously, they would've been elated to have gotten their hands on such a convenient tool to help boost the Ichise name. In the end, they would've wrung me dry." She smiled bitterly.

Hazuki could picture the fate Hana was describing. She didn't try to refute it.

And that was all there was to it.

Hazuki knew exactly what Hana was talking about.

Those so-called parents didn't have any affection toward their children.

"Well, no thanks!" Hana continued. "They'd treated me like nothing. I didn't want them to fawn over me just because I became strong. But that's the way our parents are. I didn't have a bit of faith in them. That's why I hid it. I'm positive to this day that I made the right decision.

Hana fixed Hazuki with a resolute gaze that didn't allow for any arguments. Hazuki broke under the weight of that stare and looked away.

"Then why did you reveal your secret now? If Father finds out, he's sure to order you to come back," Hazuki said.

"Who cares? I don't care what people say to me. It doesn't matter if they've all had a change of heart. It doesn't erase what they've done to me. My memories of their frosty attitudes won't disappear so easily."

"That's true..." Hazuki's face clouded over.

"What are you going to do, Hazuki?"

"What?" She looked up, startled.

"I told you, didn't I? You don't want to get married, right? Then there's only one thing you can do, no? As long as you're living under the Ichises' roof, our parents will always try to control you. I doubt that'll change once you're married to the man our shitty father chose for you, either. In fact, it might get worse for you. Do you plan to do as our parents say for the rest of your life?"

Hazuki's eyes were filled with indecision.

"You heard that the Association's headquarters was infiltrated by terrorists, right?" Hana asked.

Confused by the abrupt change in topic, Hazuki nodded. "Yeah, I heard about it. Apparently, they still haven't been found yet."

"I made a deal with Saku. I'm going to help him with the search."

"You can't. You're still a student. It's too dangerous!" Hazuki protested.

"It's okay. This isn't the first time Saku's asked something outrageous," Hana reassured her. "More importantly, as my compensation, I asked

Saku to take you in as your guardian if you decide to cut ties with the Ichise family, so you can live in the Ichinomiya residence."

Hazuki's eyes grew wide. "What are you saying?! How could you make such an exorbitant request of your husband?"

Hana snickered at Hazuki's reaction. "I knew you'd say that. But Saku agreed."

Granted, at the time, he'd smirked wickedly, looking every inch the evil villain, but Hazuki was better off not knowing that.

"So all that's left is for you to decide." Hana stepped closer to Hazuki and took her hand. "Your life is your own, just like mine is mine and no one else's."

Hazuki bit her lip and looked down. "Hana…"

"If you need me, call me," Hana said and pressed a slip of paper with her phone number into Hazuki's hand. A rueful smile rose to her face. "Isn't it strange? We're twins, but we don't even know each other's numbers. We used to be so close."

An identical smile rose to Hazuki's face. "Yeah, you're right…" She folded her fingers over the paper, holding it as if it was precious. Then without saying another word, she left the roof. There was nothing else she needed to say to Hana.

Hana wondered what Hazuki would decide.

She had to brace herself to accept whatever the outcome turned out to be, no matter if it was good or bad.

But Hana's heart felt strangely full.

"How many years has it been since we last talked like this?"

For a while, she watched the clouds pass overhead as waves of sentimentality washed over her.

Chapter 5

"No. Way."

After her conversation with her twin sister, Hana was paged through the PA system to report to the teachers' room by the third-year Class A homeroom teacher—Hazuki's homeroom teacher, in other words.

This had never happened before, and Hana had gone thinking the teacher wanted to talk about Hazuki. Instead, the discussion was about Hana.

The teacher wanted to enroll Hana in Class A.

Her answer was a no-brainer.

What was this nonsense about her situation being *sad*? Why should she have to join Class A all of a sudden?

Why did this fool think she'd worked so hard to keep her grades low enough to stay in Class C?

But even faced with Hana's ill temper and staunch rejection, he dug in his heels and refused to back down.

"I can't possibly leave a practitioner with your talents in *Class C*."

His disdain for Hana's class was obvious from the way he'd spat, "*Class C*," as if the words left a bad taste in his mouth.

Regardless of what class they were in, students were students. However, planted inside the teacher was a seed of prejudice toward Hana's classmates.

No wonder the Class C students were tormented by inferiority complexes.

It was glaringly obvious that the teachers treated the classes unequally.

"It doesn't matter what you say. No means no!" Hana yelled.

"I'm sure you dislike being in Class C, too, right, Miss Ichise?"

"Isn't that just your own biased opinion? I don't have any problems where I am."

"Nevertheless."

"Blah, blah, blah! You've turned a blind eye to all the insults muttered behind my back and the ridicule. It's too late for you to change your tune and sidle up to me!"

The Class A and B students had never gone so far as to bully her, but they had mocked her constantly, and none of the teachers—not even one—had ever come to her rescue, as if to say through their actions that being placed in Class C was a bad thing.

Hana wouldn't forget that the Class A homeroom teacher had contributed to her ridicule alongside the students.

"I'm the kind of person who will hold a grudge for life. I remember everything you've ever done, too. One day, I might just accidentally spill everything to Saku. Whoops! And he's crazy about me, you know. I can't wait to see how he'll retaliate."

Hana's glare said it all: *I'm* never *going to forget.* The teacher's face paled, and he finally shut his mouth.

"Is that all? If so, I will take my leave," she said.

He didn't try to stop her, and she rushed out of the room.

Hana had expected there to be teachers who would try this, but the experience had been even more unpleasant than she had imagined.

"If only there'd been a blunt object at hand, then I could have thrown it at his head," Hana grumbled, stomping angrily.

Arashi looked up at her with his cute, round eyes.

"Oh, Arashi. Come heal this splintered heart of mine with your pillowy soft fur!" she said and scooped Arashi up before he had a chance to say yes.

How divine was his fluff against her face? One touch, and the stormy waves crashing in her heart smoothed into gentle ripples.

She petted him until she calmed down. Then she released him again.

"Are you done?" Arashi asked.

"Yeah, thanks," she said and stroked his head.

It might be disrespectful to pet a god, but since Arashi never got angry, Hana took that as permission to do whatever she wanted.

"Geez, all this fuss just because I'm a little stronger."

"Not just 'a little.' You were strong enough to save me when I became a tatarigami. Of course it's a big deal."

"I only managed it because you hadn't lost yourself completely. And all I did was yank you out by brute force, though."

"Brute force or not, few people would have been able to accomplish such a feat. You should take more pride in yourself."

"Pride, hmm."

Hana hadn't been able to afford the luxury of going around boasting about her powers. It would have only caused a commotion, given her a headache, and put her peaceful retirement further out of reach.

But now that her secret was out in the open, she might have to start focusing on the present rather than on her retirement.

"Well, I no longer have a reason to hold myself back. That's a load off my shoulders," said Hana.

"I didn't enjoy watching them put you down, either. Aoi and Miyabi rejoice at what you did. Your impressive display has drastically cut down the number of mudslingers."

"You're right. I ought to be more like Saku, self-proclaimed genius extraordinaire." Hana snickered.

"You might yet be laughed at again depending on your grades in the upcoming exams, though?"

"Don't remind me…" Just when she'd finally forgotten about them, too.

"I don't want to hear anyone calling you strong but stupid. Please make sure it doesn't happen."

"You know, that hurts more than any of the insults hurled at me before. I don't want to hear those words coming out of anyone's mouth, either."

She now had another reason to study besides getting out of Mio's extra-special tutoring sessions.

"I'm going to eat, sleep, and breathe my studies from now on."

Hana was tired already.

◆

"Goddammit!" Saku cursed, venting his frustration by slamming his papers on his desk.

Unable to think of a good response, Hana could only watch. "You can't find them?" she asked.

"No. We haven't been able to catch a single whiff of where they could be."

It seemed that the investigation had hit a roadblock.

The location of the other stolen talismans was another concern.

The entire force of practitioners had been mobilized to help with the search, but the terrorists' whereabouts remained a mystery.

Thanks to Hana, they had been able to avoid the worst-case scenario when the school had been sieged, but there was no guarantee they would make it out unscathed next time.

Hana could see the fear in Saku's eyes over the prospect of regular people getting hurt or worse at this rate.

Why had the school been targeted in the first place?

It must have been because of the students with deep ties to the five clans: Hana and Nozomu, and the twins, Kikiyo and Kiriya.

What should they do now?

That was the hardest question at hand.

Who should answer it but Azuha?

"Master," the shikigami said to attract Hana's attention.

"What is it, Azuha?"

Since Hana had moved into the Ichinomiya residence, Azuha occasionally went out to play on her own.

That was to say, she liked to stretch her wings and explore.

Considering how powerful Azuha was, Hana figured there was little risk of her getting into trouble and let her do as she liked.

Hana had been prohibited from leaving the grounds herself, so she couldn't go on any outings with her shikigami. She was happy enough for Azuha to have a change of pace.

With her powers dampened, Azuha could pass for a normal butterfly with prettier-than-average wings.

"The group you were talking about before, the Gull of Nirvana, was it?" Azuha asked.

"The Skull of Nirvana, you mean," Hana corrected, holding back the laughter threatening to burst out.

"That's right. The Skull of Nirvana. I found them."

"What did you say?!" The outburst had come from Saku, not Hana.

He leaped toward the shikigami, looking like he meant to grab her. Hana quickly swept Azuha up to protect her.

"Don't you dare lay a hand on Azuha!" she cried.

"Focus. The Skull of Nirvana. You found them? When? Where?!" he demanded.

It was Hana's responsibility to rein in his zeal. She picked up the giant squeaky hammer she'd recently bought online and smacked him on the shin with all her might.

"Uck—!"

Hana shot a cold glare at Saku, who was writhing in pain, and gently asked Azuha, "How did you find them?"

"Oh, I was flying through the sky, and I saw a bunch of people talking on a roof—they wore the mark of the Skull and Spider Lily," answered the shikigami.

"Do you remember where that was?"

"Nope."

Saku's shoulders slumped when he heard that. "Ah."

"Oh, oh! But you said Master shouldn't go outside until the bad men are caught, and I wanted to help, so I brainwashed them." Azuha casually dropped that bomb in her usual sweet voice.

Saku's face twitched. "Wait, what do you mean, 'brainwashed'?"

"I hypnotized them to attack Master," she replied proudly. "If you can't find them, then have them come to you. That'll make them easy to catch, right?"

"S-sure."

Azuha had no clue that she'd done something outrageous. She held no malicious intent. She'd only wanted to help Hana.

"So I'm pretty sure they're going to come for Master sometime soon."

Normally, Hana should have scolded Azuha for the stunt she had pulled. However, Azuha, having seen the actual culprits, must have judged that Hana would be able to handle them. Otherwise, she wouldn't have intentionally put Hana in harm's way.

"Azuha was a good girl, Master?" Azuha asked innocently.

"Mm-hmm. You're amazing, Azuha. You did so well," Hana said.

"Ahem. I *am* your shikigami, after all," she boasted, fluttering around the room.

"What's with all your shikigami?" asked Saku despairingly with his head buried in his arms. "Aren't they a little too far out of the box?"

Hana wasn't sure how to answer him, either. Even she was surprised that Azuha had come back, casual as ever, after brainwashing the terrorists they'd been breaking their backs to find.

Having been forewarned by Azuha that the Skull of Nirvana was going to make their move soon, Hana and Saku decided to go out in the open…on dates.

If Hana hunkered down in the heavily guarded Ichinomiya residence, the terrorists wouldn't be able to strike even if they wanted to.

To lure them out, she had to make the first move.

That was why she and Saku were going out alone to bait their enemies with what looked to be a juicy opportunity.

Of course, the Association's practitioners were hiding out of sight, charged with Hana's protection. They were so thorough at their job that even Hana, their ward, couldn't tell where they were.

Saku and Hana spent a few successive days wandering around isolated places, and yet they saw neither hide nor hair of the terrorists.

At first, Hana had constantly been on edge, never knowing when the attack would come, but gradually, she lowered her guard.

The complete and utter lack of movement had Saku asking, "Are they really coming?"

"You don't believe in Azuha's abilities?" Hana retorted. "Okay, yes, but there seriously isn't a single sign that they're planning to strike." She sighed.

The two of them were sitting on a bench in a nearly deserted park.

"Well, at least I get to enjoy these dates. That's a nice perk," Saku said, his demeanor becoming flirtier.

Hana started to back away, but his arm wrapped around her waist. "Wait, Saku. We're outside!" she protested.

"No one's here. What's the problem?"

He stroked her lip with his thumb. A shiver ran down her spine.

"Well, Hana? I've made my feelings for you clear. Isn't it time you give in and accept them?"

Thrown off-balance, she hissed, "Is this the time?" Her face was bright red.

"You're the first person I've wanted so badly. And you like me, too, no?"

"No. No, no, no."

She turned away, unable to bear the heat in Saku's gaze, but he grabbed her chin and forced her to face him again.

There was nowhere to run.

She had come to hate that brazen smile of his, but she couldn't look away, either.

"Don't hide. I want to know how you feel. Do you hate me?" Saku asked.

Hana stammered, unable to get out a coherent word, but Saku refused to let her off the hook.

"Hana," he said. "You don't have to say anything. If you don't want it, turn away." He leaned in closer.

I have to turn away. But I can't.

Alarm bells were ringing in her head. She had to decide now, or he was going to kiss her.

But did she *hate* Saku? She…

When Hana showed no signs of dodging even though their lips were a mere breath apart, the corner of Saku's lips quirked upward. He started to close the final distance between them. That was when it happened.

"Don't you dare move any closer!!"

Hana jumped at the loud yell. She regained her senses and shoved Saku away.

"Agh—!" Saku barely stopped himself from tumbling off the bench. "Damn. I was so close," he cursed in frustration.

His words made Hana blush. She turned to look at the interlopers instead.

"Kikiyo. Kiriya. What are you doing here?"

The loud protest that had stopped the kiss had come from Kikiyo. Her eyes welling, she wrapped herself around Hana. "We're in on the plan. We came along to protect you!"

"Y-you were watching?"

Heat rose to Hana's cheeks when she realized the twins had seen the entire exchange.

Now she remembered. That was right. Other practitioners were hiding in the shadows.

The thought that everyone had been watching her and Saku made her want to dig a hole and bury herself in it.

"Thank god I saved you from the wolf."

Kikiyo didn't seem like she had any intention of leaving Hana's side. But wasn't Saku the one she liked?

Hana couldn't help but think that Kikiyo was focused on the wrong person.

"Hey! What the hell are you butting in for?" Saku demanded.

"It's not proper of you to push yourself on Hana when she doesn't want it. It's indecent!" yelled Kikiyo.

"What's wrong with a husband kissing his wife?!" he shot back. "Hold on, aren't you supposed to be angry at Hana, not me?"

It was exactly like he said. Kikiyo liked Saku, so if she was going to take offense, it should've been with Hana kissing Saku.

"Well, then marry me!" Kikiyo demanded.

"No way!"

Before, Kikiyo had been too embarrassed to tell Saku how she felt, but apparently, she had flung her shame out the window.

Never mind that Saku had shot down her brazen proposal point-blank.

"You're the worst! You don't have to be so rude about it." Kikiyo glued herself to Hana and whined, "Hanaaa."

"Don't cling on to her. She's mine," Saku shouted, peeling the Nijouin twin off Hana.

She lashed out at him. "Wrong! Hana belongs to everyone."

"Um, no, I belong to myself," Hana said.

Saku and Kikiyo argued back and forth. There wasn't a trace of Kikiyo's supposed affection for Saku to be seen. Hana tilted her head in confusion, wondering what was going on.

Kiriya said to her softly, "Back in our last school, the other students kept their distance since we're candidates to be the next-generation head of the Nijouin clan. Kikiyo couldn't make any friends. That's why she's so happy to be friends with you. She still has some feelings for Saku, but you're more important to her, it seems."

As he explained—in full sentences, no less—he watched Kikiyo warmly. He added, "Please continue to take care of her." He bowed deeply for the umpteenth time,

Hana smiled ruefully. "I'll do what I can."

◆

Kikiyo and Kiriya ended up joining them, so they were going to be spending the rest of the day as a group of four. Saku had been enjoying the date, so his mood plummeted. Occasionally, he tsked in disapproval.

By contrast, Kikiyo was in high spirits. "It's almost noon. Let's get out of here and go eat lunch!"

"I could eat," Hana said.

"The Nijouins run a restaurant nearby. I can personally guarantee the quality."

"Okay… Oh, but let me run to the bathroom before we go," Hana said. "Wait here."

"I'll go with you," Kikiyo said.

The two of them went off to a public restroom a short distance away.

When they were done, they stepped back outside to find a group of clearly suspicious individuals encircling the bathroom. It looked like they had been waiting for Hana and Kikiyo.

Hana immediately had her guard up. She noticed that a barrier surrounded them, one that looked identical to the barrier that had been put up around the school when it had been overrun by shades. She checked her phone, and the signal was jammed.

On top of that, when she looked really closely at the goons surrounding them, she noticed they all had buttons engraved with a skull-and-spider-lily design, just like Saku had said.

"You're with the Gull of Nirvana?" Hana asked.

"It's the Skull of Nirvana, Hana," Kikiyo corrected instantly.

"Whoops. That's right."

No matter how many times Hana had taught Azuha otherwise, the shikigami persisted in saying, "Gull," and Hana had unintentionally parroted the mistake.

"You must be the wife of the Ichinomiya clan head, Hana Ichise. Come with us," one of the assailants demanded.

"Are you the person in charge?" Hana asked.

"Exactly! I am the leader. It would have been impolite to send subordinates to greet the lady of the clan."

"Well, thank you for your courtesy. But *you're* the ones who will be coming with *us*."

Azuha flew off from where she sat in Hana's hair and fluttered over the Skull of Nirvana members.

They dismissed her as a regular butterfly. Big mistake.

Azuha flapped her wings, showering them with fine scales. A portion of the group, probably the ones Azuha had brainwashed before, peeled away and started to attack their own allies.

"What—what do you think you're doing?!" Rattled by the sudden attack, the boss of the terrorists twisted his head, looking around in confusion.

Azuha swooped again. The eyes of the underlings around him took on a vacant look. They swayed toward him and seized him by his arms.

"Stop!" he hollered. "What are you doing?! *She's* the one you're supposed to capture!"

As he struggled in his captors' grips, Miyabi prowled up behind him with the squeaky hammer in hand. She smiled angelically, raised the giant hammer high, and slammed it down on his head.

"Urk—!"

There was nothing toylike about the sound the hammer made when it struck his skull. His eyes rolled back, and he collapsed.

"Oof, that must've hurt."

"He had it coming."

They had taken down the top dog with no trouble at all. Kikiyo began to search his prone body, discovering a small treasure trove of objects, one after another.

"Could those be the missing talismans?" Hana asked.

"Yeah. Apparently, he was carrying them all on his person. Including the ones we found in our school, the count matches perfectly."

"Sweet. So case closed?"

"Yes. That was so easy, it makes me wonder why we went through all that trouble." Despite their victory, Kikiyo's expression was complicated. "We should have asked for your help from the start..." She was despondent when she should've been rejoicing.

"I'm good at physical labor. Anyway, we solved the case, so let's consider it a win." Hana patted Kikiyo's shoulder consolingly. "I'm going to break the barrier."

"All right," Kikiyo said.

Hana prepared to launch into a kick at the barrier when Miyabi stopped her. "Master, let me take care of it." The shikigami shot her a dazzling smile and brandished the toy hammer, brimming with enthusiasm.

Hana had bought the toy online on a whim, but it seemed Miyabi had taken a liking to it. She had imbued it with her power and turned it into her personal weapon. She was looking for the chance to test its might.

Hana gave her the green light. "Okay, go ahead."

"Yes, ma'am," Miyabi said brightly. She faced the barrier and swung the hammer *hard*.

The barrier broke with a sound like shattering glass.

Aoi and Arashi had long since taken out the boss's underlings. None were left standing.

Instead, several people who looked like practitioners came dashing out of the overgrown field.

"Are you unharmed?"

"We're sorry we're late! The Skull of Nirvana attacked us out of nowhere. The fighting is still ongoing, and the surroundings are in disarray. Lord Ichinomiya is grappling with the assailants as well."

"Ah, I see," Hana said. That was why no one had come to their rescue.

Saku would have noticed when the barrier had gone up. Was the situation so bad that he couldn't be spared to help?

"Kikiyo, I'm going to join Saku."

"My priority is ensuring the retrieval of the talismans," Kikiyo said.

"Got it. Be careful. It looks like the Skull of Nirvana guys are still around."

Kikiyo nodded. "Okay. You too, Hana."

As Hana headed in Saku's direction, she commanded her shikigami. "You guys go support the practitioners fighting in the area."

"Will do," Aoi said, and the four of them scattered.

Hana headed straight for where she'd left Saku. But when she got there...

"Idiots! You've got some guts thinking you can challenge me with your piddling power," Saku roared.

"Eeeeek! We're sorry. So, so, so, so, so sorry!"

"Please spare us!"

It seemed Hana needn't have bothered coming to help. The enemies were more banged up than Saku was and had already moved on to begging for their lives.

"Do you know how much trouble you've caused me?" Saku snapped. "Save your pleading for when you meet your maker."

"Eyaaaagh!"

The men had already lost all will to fight back, but Saku whaled on them anyway. Watching him, Hana felt her cheek twitch.

He must have been nursing quite the grudge against the terrorist group. At this rate, he really was going to send them straight into the next life.

Kiriya came up behind Saku and pinned his arms down to hold him back.

"Come on, Saku, what are you doing?" Hana said.

"Hana. You took care of things on your end?"

"If you have the time to be playing around, shouldn't you have helped me? Granted, you would've been too late anyway. Azuha and Miyabi took down the boss in a heartbeat."

"That's what I figured would happen, which is why I didn't go. But maybe I should have if the leader was there. What did you do with him?"

"Handed him over first thing to the practitioners who were guarding us."

Saku clicked his tongue. "Damn. I missed my chance."

What was he planning to have done if he had gotten there in time?

Maybe it was a good thing, at least for the leader, that Miyabi had mowed him down instantly.

And so the whole affair drew to a disappointing end.

Kiriya went after Kikiyo. Hana could relax. All there was left to do was wait for her shikigami to come back.

Then from a short distance away came an explosion of malevolent energy.

Hana became alert and turned to look in the direction it was coming from, unease rising within her. "Saku, what—?" she bit out.

"Come on. We're going!" Saku ran for the origin of the sinister energy.

Hana hurried after him.

Farther inside the park, there was a plaza where a concentrated mound of purple goop was busy slurping up its victims. A few people were still free. They looked like members of the Skull of Nirvana.

"Gyaaah!"

"Help! Save us!"

They screamed desperately as they fled toward Hana, but they, too, were snatched up by the malicious entity.

Hana took the scene in and froze. "What is that?"

"Shit! They went and triggered the nastiest of the stolen talismans."

"What?! But Kikiyo said the boss had been carrying all of them!"

That was when her phone rang. It was Kikiyo—her timing was impeccable.

Hana picked up. "Hello? Kikiyo?"

"I'm so sorry, Hana! I recounted the talismans, and there's one missing! It's the most dangerous one, too! Just our luck."

"It was activated just a second ago."

"That's bad news. We're heading back right now!"

They hung up.

Hana's shikigami returned from separate corners of the park. They had sensed the abnormality.

"Master!" Aoi cried.

"What is that, Master?" Miyabi asked.

"Even if you ask me, I have no clue," Hana said. She looked to Saku for an answer. "Saku?"

His expression was stark. "That talisman sucks up people with powers nearby and uses their energy to summon shades. The more people it eats up, the stronger the shades it can bring forth."

"Excuse me?! What kind of useless skill is that?!"

"Don't ask me that. A practitioner from the Nijouin clan made it long ago," he said. "Look. The shades are already gathering."

The shades that had come oozing out of the brickwork were the strongest Hana had ever encountered.

"Bind!" Saku shouted, trapping both the purple sludge and the shades it had summoned in a barrier together. "At least this will contain the talisman's energy so it can't attract any more shades."

"But what do we do about the talisman? Ah— Whoa!" As they were chatting, a shade in the swarm struck out at Hana. She evaded the attack by a hairbreadth.

Aoi instantly cleaved the offending shade in half.

But what in the world was this? The halves morphed into separate shades.

"What just happened?!" Hana screamed.

"It's the talisman's doing. The shades are drawing power from that ball of malignant energy," Saku explained. "The situation's only going to get worse unless we do something about the talisman."

"You can't be serious."

What in the world was that Nijouin practitioner thinking when they made the talisman?

Had they been standing in front of Hana, she wouldn't have been satisfied until she'd punched them at least three times.

"Saku, what do we do?"

"I don't know!" he admitted honestly.

Hana's eyes looked hollow. "What?!"

"What do you want from me? The talisman is so dangerous that it's never been used. The only person who knows how to deal with it is the inventor."

"And you have the nerve to call yourself lord of the Ichinomiya clan!" she complained to Saku while fending off the onslaught. Her expression was twisted with panic. "How do we fix this?"

At the moment, she and Saku were only dragging things out until they completely exhausted themselves.

The Nijouin twins might have a solution, but would they arrive in time?

As she agonized over what to do, Arashi kicked down a shade coming right at her and came over. "You have the means to dispose of it, do you not, Hana?"

"Huh?"

"It's a similar tactic to the one you used to save me. Pull out the victims, seal the talisman in a barrier, and stamp out its energy."

Arashi didn't look entirely confident, either, but Hana couldn't keep doing nothing. "I got it. I'll give it a try."

"I've got your back," Arashi promised.

Hana slowly approached the talisman, which was enveloped by its shroud of dark energy. She laid a hand on the mass while weaving a powerful barrier to contain it.

Tendrils of energy curled around her, trying to suck her in, but thanks to her barrier, she was safe.

Hana followed Arashi's instructions and sent forth her own energy to peel the victims away from the glob.

The talisman seemed to writhe in pain and redoubled its efforts to trap her.

Hana's barrier buckled minutely.

Hana was taken aback. Realizing that she didn't have time to waste, she worked quickly to pour her power throughout the mass, manipulating it carefully to look for the boundaries between the talisman and the trapped people. When she found one, she aimed her energy at the divide, freeing the victims of the malignant shroud one by one. None of them were moving, but she had no time to check if they were alive.

Hana broke into a cold sweat.

Unlike the time she had saved Arashi, quantity, not quality, was required. She reached out with her power carefully, making sure the talisman was able to push her back a bit.

She kept one eye on the people she'd freed. She could feel the talisman's attempts to fight her off growing more and more desperate.

The talisman lashed out violently in one final act of frenzied resistance. Hana threw everything she had into countering the attack.

The barrier around Hana shattered nearly the same instant she ripped out the final victim.

Suddenly deprived of its power source, the talisman suppressed the dark energy it had been emitting. In the end, all that was left behind was a silver rod that could fit in the palm of one's hand.

Even in its diminished state, it was still trying to suck Hana in. She wasted no time in sealing it under several layers of barriers.

The malice in the air dissipated. When Aoi cut through a shade with a broad swing of his great sword, it died without regenerating. "Ah, good, they're killable again."

From then on, it was the shikigamis' show. They were back in familiar territory where they reigned undefeated.

Hana watched the shades being cut down one after another and sighed heavily. "God, I'm exhausted…"

◆

Hana gave the last of the stolen talismans to Kikiyo when the other girl returned, who looked shocked to receive it; the question *Were you the one to seal it away?* filled her eyes.

But Hana didn't have the energy to explain.

She could barely walk. Saku scooped her up and carried her to the car.

They set off. Hana leaned heavily against Saku as she stared out at the passing scenery.

"Saku, I'm sleepy…," she said.

"Sleep. I'll handle the rest," Saku replied.

"Mmkay…"

Hana drifted off. The next time she woke up, two days had already come and gone.

She opened her eyes and saw Aoi and Miyabi hovering over her. Their worried expressions eased when they saw her stir.

"Thank goodness, Master," Miyabi said.

"You gave us a scare," Aoi added reproachfully. "You weren't waking up at all."

"Sorry," Hana said, petting Aoi's head. He looked embarrassed but made no move to stop her.

"I'm sorry to bother you when you've just woken up, but you received several calls while you were sleeping," Miyabi told her.

"Calls?" Hana took her phone, which Miyabi was holding out, and checked the notifications. They were all from an unknown number.

Was this what they called twin telepathy?

Hana instinctively knew that Hazuki had been the caller, and she dialed her sister back.

Several days after Hana had recovered her strength, she paid a visit to the Ichise house.

Sae greeted her with a happy expression. "Welcome home, Miss Hana."

"Where are they?" Hana asked.

"Please come with me."

Hana followed Sae through the main building of her family home, feeling nostalgic but not sentimental. Sae guided her to the room her parents were in.

She hadn't told her parents in advance that she'd be coming, and they were horribly astonished by her sudden appearance.

"What have you come for, ungrateful child?!" her father yelled.

Her mother sniffed haughtily. "It's too late for you to cry for forgiveness. No doubt you were driven out of the Ichinomiya residence, but there is no place for you here. We won't take you in even if you beg to come back."

Her parents were far from being delighted at her homecoming. Instead, the first words out of their mouths were venomous and reproachful.

Hana snorted. "There's no way I would ever want to return to this house. Where in the world do you get your baseless confidence? How idiotic." Her smirk was thoroughly scornful.

Her father's face reddened with anger. "How dare you speak to your parents with such disrespect!" he exploded.

"Don't go calling yourselves my parents when you've never acted like parents!" she shouted back.

"Wha—?!"

Come to think of it, this might have been the first time Hana had ever talked back to her parents.

Up until now, she had always listened to their cutting remarks without saying anything. They must have thought of her as mousy and docile.

What a laugh.

"I didn't come to move back in. I came to say good-bye for good," Hana said.

"What do you mean, 'for good'?" asked her father.

Hana leveled a frosty, dispassionate gaze at her puzzled parents.

Just then, Hazuki came into the room.

"Oh, Hazuki, did you need something?" their mother asked.

"Come. You talk some sense into your sister," their father said. "This ungrateful, no-good daughter won't pay her flesh-and-blood parents our due. Teach her to know her place."

"You're the ones who have forgotten your place," Hazuki retorted.

"What did you say?"

"Hana is currently the wife of the Ichinomiya lord. Who do you think should be bowing to whom? Even the youngest children of the five clans' branch families know the answer to that."

This could be called Hazuki's first act of resistance against their parents.

Their parents' eyes bulged out of their heads with disbelief. Their expressions were so hilarious that it was physically painful for Hana to hold back her laughter.

"What's gotten into you, Hazuki? For you to join your sister in her madness…"

"Father, Mother, today, I have something to say to you," Hazuki said calmly.

"What is it?"

Their parents composed themselves in response to Hazuki's collected demeanor and paused to listen.

Hazuki declared with a smile, "I will not marry the person you picked out for me, Father."

Silence fell over the room. Their father didn't seem to register what Hazuki had said at first, but after a minute, his face flushed red with rage. "What nonsense is this?! The date for the ceremony has already been decided."

Exactly as Hana had predicted. She'd figured that once the families were formally introduced to each other, their parents would be eager to marry off Hazuki as soon as possible, and apparently, they were really planning on going through with it.

She had thought her opinion of their parents had already hit rock bottom, but it now sunk even further.

"You decided that all on your own. I want to choose the person I marry," Hazuki said.

"Don't be so selfish! We already told you this marriage is crucial for the family. You only have to do as we say!" their father snapped.

Hazuki felt hopeless and resigned, her face falling like her last hope had been crushed.

Hana wanted to step in, but she held herself back; this wasn't the time for her to interfere.

Hazuki's expression was forlorn, but a bright light shone in her eyes. She met their parents' gazes head-on.

"I have obeyed your instructions all this time. Everything was for our family's sake, for Father and Mother's sake, for Hana's sake. That's what I always believed."

Their father's face lit up. "And that is precisely right. See, you *do* understand."

Hazuki glared back at him. "But I've had enough!"

The thunder of her voice filled the room. *Even the people outside the room must have heard*, Hana thought as she listened for Hazuki's next words.

"I suppressed my desires and worked myself to the bone all for Hana! You said you would put her up for adoption, so I convinced myself I had to do her share and did as you said. But you've pushed me too far! Hana's left the house, and now you're trying to marry me off to a man I hardly know."

Hazuki's vehemence rendered their parents speechless. They stared at her wide-eyed.

Hazuki wasn't done. "Father, and you too, Mother, all you think about is the Ichise name. Have you ever thought of us as your children? Not even once, right? To you, your children are nothing more than convenient tools at your disposal. Don't saddle us with your inferiority complexes just because neither of you have any talent."

Their father looked like he wanted to rebut Hazuki's argument, but the words seemed to be stuck in his throat. His mouth opened and closed soundlessly.

Hazuki's first act of rebellion.

It was their duty to swallow it.

"I'm leaving this house. I've already packed."

Outside the room were three large suitcases.

When their father saw them, the fact that Hazuki was serious must have hit home. Panicked, he spat, "We won't let you!"

"I don't need your permission. I might be a student, but I'm legally of age. I don't want to stay with people like you who care so little for me."

Hazuki took a suitcase in each hand and looked to Hana for help with the third. "Can you carry the last one for me?" she asked.

"Mm-hmm, of course." Hana picked it up.

The two of them turned identical smiles on their parents, looking like the twins they were.

"Farewell, shitty geezer."

"Farewell, damn hag."

With those final words, they shut the door and fled the house before their parents could chase after them, giggling all the way.

"I wish you both happiness, Miss Hana and Miss Hazuki." Sae smiled at them warmly and waved after them.

Hana and Hazuki climbed into the Ichinomiya car and left the Ichise house behind them.

Saku was waiting for them back at the Ichinomiya residence.

"I'm Hazuki Ichise! I'll be imposing on you from today on," Hazuki said, introducing herself.

"Saku Ichinomiya. Welcome. Make yourself at home."

"All right! Thank you."

Hana was glad to see Hazuki's radiant smile.

She felt as if she had slipped back into a moment from the past.

The shadows had receded from Hazuki's face.

The twins' hands were clasped tightly together just like when they were young.